Caught in the backwater eddies of a small Texas town in the hot summer of 1943, a handful of ordinary people—an attractive divorcee, her two small sons, a brash, handsome sailor, a mute and crippled handyman—join in the tightly woven drama of this extraordinary story.

Shadowed by the specter of World War II, the strands of a woman's desires, a child's needs, and a man's fears uncoil into an unusual, sensitive love story. But with the suddenness of a snapped spring, an explosion of hidden yearnings, unexpected passions, and murderous hatreds culminates in a bloody, terror-filled night of violence and death.

This compelling tale boils with action and nail-biting suspense and with the warmth and humor generated by characters as real as the people we know. When the last page of *Raggedy Man* is turned, we can see the most important part of it all: the gentle regenerative power of the human spirit. Don't be surprised if it brings a tear to your eye and a smile to your lips.

Also by William D. Wittliff and Sara Clark
THADDEUS ROSE & EDDIE

RAGGEDY MAN

William D. Wittliff
& Sara Clark

PINNACLE BOOKS   LOS ANGELES

RAGGEDY MAN

Copyright © 1979 by William D. Wittliff

An original Pinnacle Books edition, published for the first time anywhere.

First printing, July 1979

ISBN: 0-523-40406-9

Cover illustration by Norm Eastman

Printed in the United States of America

PINNACLE BOOKS, INC.
2029 Century Park East
Los Angeles, California 90067

For the woman who was Nita
and the boy who was Harry

1

Nita Longley stood at the sunburned front screen, with all the other doors open in a row behind her, pushing the damp curls off her neck and trying to coax a scrap of breeze under the low ceiling of her "shotgun house." The not-quite-respectable-sounding name—shotgun house—was part of the reason she disliked this run-down place she shared with her two boys.

The Southwest Consolidated Telephone Company, which also shared it, was another reason. Not only did it own the house and the pay telephone on the front-room wall behind her and the octopus-armed switchboard beyond that, in the middle room; it also owned her—or tried to. When she thought of the telephone company, she saw herself as a tiny blonde mouse, soft, helpless and stupid, trapped in this paint-peeled, Texas coastal-flatland house, while outside the flimsy doors and loose, rattling windows lurked the giant, relentless Consolidated Telephone cat.

The year was 1943. Besides the telephone company, there was also a war lurking outside her shotgun house.

Through the screen, Nita watched the crippled handyman, Mr. Bailey, his head bobbing with his limp as he pushed his ancient steel-wheeled lawnmower down the middle of the road. She pulled back out of the sunlit doorway into the shadow of the airless, pink-walled front room where he couldn't see her. It wasn't just the way he looked, with his face so scarred that she always glanced away without meeting his eyes, or the fact that he couldn't talk and she never knew what to say to him.

It was also, somehow, that he reminded her of herself.

As he clattered toward her like a tone-deaf, one-man band with the long-handled rake and shovel and hoe banging, wired to the arm of the mower, she read in his lurching steps the story of her own inept and faltering attempts to make a life, a good life, for herself and the boys. Mr. Bailey reminded her that things could go terribly wrong, that circumstances could cripple, and the best of her plans and hopes could wither on the vine, useless, yellow.

The real truth was that sometimes she was afraid they already had. With a shiver, she watched the rusty array of clippers, pliers, screwdrivers, files, and hammers, swinging frantically in crazy arcs from the loops in Mr. Bailey's homemade toolbelt. Worn-out, corroded, broken, defective . . .

What was the thing she should have done differently, the one that would've made everything else come out all right? Why had the bright and translucent future turned the corner into what she saw now as the dark, regretted past? Nita sighed. Was it the divorce? Her sister-in-law had said she'd live to regret it. But it had seemed so much better than the turbulent river of bitter arguments they had tried to steer through for so long. Was it leaving Philipsville after the divorce and coming here with the two little boys in her arms? But she'd been so thankful at finding the job, any job to support them, after looking so long, being told no so often. . . . She saw Mr. Bailey glance up once toward the door and then quickly back down to his lawnmower. Was it *her* embarrassment that triggered his? Often she was aware, as she directed her attention pointedly away from him, that he turned his disfigured face and busied himself with something at his feet whenever she was near. He was as uncomfortable in her presence as she was in his.

Nita sighed. Beyond Mr. Bailey's bobbing head, there where the road met the highway, she could see the houses where the town really began, the town that, like the rest of the bright world outside her shotgun house, she hadn't visited for months.

Craning her neck, she could see Francine Lucas's window with its tiny single-starred flag still in place. Poor Francine. Nita had taken the dreaded call just last week: dead, Francine's son, Emile, his aircraft carrier in the Pacific, Japanese bombs, no survivors. . . . In spite of the heavy midday heat, Nita felt a chill move along her spine as she recalled Francine's stricken face, her anguished bawl.

Only a week ago, Emile, who had delivered drugstore medicines on his bike until he was old enough to join up, had been alive, breathing, moving, laughing . . . and his poor mother, Francine, not yet impaled through the heart on her proud double-winged Army Air Corps pin. Only a week ago.

A flashy, fiery instant, and the future became the past: Emile was dead; his mother, terribly wounded. A week had passed since that instant and Nita stood here now at the door in the airless pink-walled shadow of the front room, remembering. . . .

It would be another week before Nita's own sharp-toothed flaring instant, raging with fear and death, became her suddenly closed-mouth past. Then she wouldn't recall at all that she had stood here this sunburned, sunshafted few minutes, thinking of Emile, hiding from Mr. Bailey's one good eye. Crouched in the hot darkness of her shotgun house *that* awful night, breathless, listening, Nita would be able to think only of the very real shotgun heavy in her damp-palmed hand, while her two little boys huddled beside her and the cut wires of the switchboard coiled limply before them on the floor. Terror would fill her mouth with sand and her ears with the thunder of the shotgun blast that would shred the night and their lives beyond repair. The week would pass. There could be no turning back.

Years later, after she had moved away and

4

was trying to forget the terrible things that happened here, she learned that the name "shotgun house" came simply from the cheap way these clapboard crackerboxes were built, the rooms set one behind the other like boxcars on a derailed train. When she could once again think about this house without a shudder of horror, she heard that they said you could blast a shotgun clean through from the front porch to the back stoop, if all the doors were open in between, and that's where the name came from —nothing more sinister than that. A faded red wooden-sided cattle truck rattled past behind Mr. Bailey on the road in front of the house, with a sharp-nosed white blur of a face at the window, startling Nita's thoughts back from Emile and Francine to the sunny afternoon. She watched the truck through the cloud of dust it stirred up—everyone going someplace, everyone but her.

"Somewhere over the rainbow" hummed through her head.

Her son Harry wheeled uncertainly around the porch on the blue Schwinn bike, much too big for him, that Mr. Bailey had found somewhere one day and pushed into the yard as a gift. Careening at a 45-degree angle, Harry narrowly missed the overturned red wagon and steered an uncertain arc around the corner of the house.

Nita looked around the yard for her younger son Henry before she spied his small, dusty, sunbrowned feet hanging quietly above her head among the limbs and leaves of the chinaberry tree by the porch.

"Mr. Bailey!" he yelled excitedly from his leafy perch.

The handyman rolled the lawnmover into the yard, grinning crookedly.

The pair of bare feet overhead wiggled and squirmed until Henry's faded overall pants legs were also visible under the chinaberry limbs. Suddenly his short chunky body swung into view, hung precariously by one arm for an instant, kicking and then crash-landing in the dust five feet below.

"Hey, Mr. Bailey!" he repeated happily.

Nita watched Henry dust off his overalls and wondered if he even noticed that the poor old handyman never spoke.

She had already half-turned away from the door when the rasping buzz, the voice of the switchboard that governed her life, the sound she woke to every morning and the last thing she heard at night, called her to the middle room. She walked into the pink-tinged gloom, past the plush couch, slick-armed, sagging its maroon cushions against the linoleum, and past the round-topped old radio in the corner under the whatnot shelf that bore her only treasures: the white lacy china basket, filled with brightly painted china eggs, that Walter had bought for her at the State Fair in Dallas before they were married ("State Fair 1934" it said in gold paint on the side), and the tin-framed photo of the boys and himself that Walter had made at Montgomery's Studio for her Christmas present the year before the divorce. The buzzing called her past the only other things in the front room: the pay telephone, mounted on the interior wall, and the straight-backed chair that stood formally beside it.

"Number please," she recited, picking up the headset and plugging in a wiry arm of the blinking-eyed switchboard that gripped her in its web here in the middle room.

"Thirty-seven? . . . Just a moment, I'll connect you."

She sighed.

Outside the window, beyond the arched back of the Southwest Consolidated Telephone cat, lurked that greater carnivore, the war, which lashed and growled across the face of the world.

Nita rubbed her hand across her eyes as she waited for the caller to finish. It was the war, the same war that had snatched up Emile Lucas in its flaming teeth and flung Francine sprawling in agony. That same war had a hold of them all and wouldn't let go. It was the war, she knew, that held her and Harry and Henry fast in its invisible jaws, held them miserable, green, and dying, as surely as Emile had died. The war was everywhere . . . and no one escaped.

"Birds fly o-ver the rain-bow," hummed through her mind. "Why, then, *oh why*, can't I?"

2

Outside, a little embarrassed at not landing on his feet when he jumped from the tree, Henry grinned at Mr. Bailey, who nodded and half-smiled out of the one side of his mouth that worked. Henry had discussed with Harry the fact that only half of everything about Mr. Bailey worked right: only one of his arms and one of his legs, only half of his mouth. Close scrutiny had convinced them that only one of his eyes had an eyeball, and even that was squinted almost shut. He couldn't talk at all.

Maybe he fell out of a tree, Henry had guessed. Or off of a bike, Harry had wondered. Maybe he got hurt in the war, they both speculated. They knew enough not to ask.

"You gonna mow the dirt today, Mr. Bailey?" Henry asked, pulling up his shirtless hand-me-down overalls.

Mr. Bailey half-smiled and nodded, as Harry

emerged from around the corner of the house, struggling to keep the bike upright, his sharp features screwed up with the effort of concentration. At the sight of Mr. Bailey, his face relaxed into a grin, and the bike immediately fell over in a rusted heap, dumping Harry in the dirt.

"I'm Okay," he said, exasperated, sitting up as Mr. Bailey hobbled toward him. Riding a bike was a lot harder than he had figured from watching other kids. He grinned at Mr. Bailey. "Hi," he said. "Yard day?"

Again Mr. Bailey nodded as he turned the handlebars around and stood the bike up, checking the front wheel.

"Well," Henry announced, "I gotta get back up in my tree, Mr. Bailey." He ran to the chinaberry trunk and began to shinny up to the lowest limb.

From inside came the buzz of the switchboard.

Mr. Bailey looked up from the slightly askew bike wheel, glanced at Harry's blond head bent over the loose fender, and squinted under Henry's dangling feet. His one good eye peered past the SOUTHWEST CONSOLIDATED TELEPHONE COMPANY sign tacked to the 2 x 4 porch post, to the open door, and into the pink-stained darkness beyond. He knew she was somewhere inside.

Seated at the switchboard where she could answer its demands, headset in place, Nita was filling the old black fountain pen from the well in the side of the ink bottle. She placed a sheet of lined white paper on the desk in front of her and then chewed the pen for several minutes.

Francine's face rose up before her, red-blotched and tear-stained, and Nita took the pen out of her mouth. It had to be today, even with no idea yet what she was going to write.

"Dear Judge," she began and stopped. After several more minutes she went on.

"Here is my situation." It was difficult saying all this to a perfect stranger, a judge, no less.

"I am a divorced woman with two little boys, ages six and eight," she finally wrote. *"Their names are Henry and Harry, Henry is the little one."*

She stopped again and thought a few minutes before she went on. *"For two years I have run this telephone office here in Gregory. They pay me 35 dollars a month, which is not enough to keep . . ."*

When the eye of the switchboard lit up again, Nita dropped her pen and unplugged the cord to disconnect the call.

Looking down at the letter, she tried to remember what she'd been saying. Oh yes, *". . . not enough to keep . . ."* She picked up her pen. *". . . a bird alive, let alone a woman and two little boys. To make ends meet I have to work the night shift as well as the day shift. This brings in another 20 dollars a month. I am sure I could find a better job, but the thing is I am told by my boss, Mr. John T. Rigby, that I am frozen to this one because of the war. He says it would be breaking the law for me to try to find another one. The grocer here, Mr.*

Buford, told me to write you, that you had influence and might be willing to help me get unfrozen from this job so that I can look for a better one. I hope you will take this matter up with the Texas Employment Agency on my behalf. I know things are bad all over because of the war and everybody needs to work. Well, I am not afraid to work . . ."

When the switchboard buzzed again, she wrote faster. *". . . but we can't go on living like this. Yours truly, Nita Longley."* There—it was done!

The buzzing stopped as she plugged in the cord.

"Number please . . ."

The eyes of the switchboard stared balefully at her. There were scratching noises outside the window.

"Just a moment, please. I'll connect you."

3

From his lookout post in the chinaberry tree, Henry could see a long way in all directions. He could see the cow in the bushy lot across the road. He could see the houses that began where the road met the highway and piled up closer to each other as his eye moved toward where he knew "town" was, there below the Methodist church steeple and the waterbank, where the 280 souls of Gregory, Texas, met for spiritual and commercial exchange.

Town was a strange place. Henry couldn't remember living anywhere else, but he sure had the feeling Gregory wasn't where they belonged. For one thing, there weren't many kids to play with. Harry knew a few boys from school, but one of them, dark-eyed Berto Zamora, lived on the other side of town, farther than Nita let them wander, and others lived completely out in the country, beyond all hope of visiting.

Once, down by the barbershop, they had run into a group of older boys, barefoot on dusty bikes, who had thrown rocks at them and called them "orphans."

"You ain't got no daddy!" one of the boys had yelled at them as he let fly a rock that had hit the wagonload of groceries they were pulling home.

"Tell Mama it fell out and broke," Harry had cautioned as he and Henry examined the bottle of milk smashed inside the bag, after they had pulled the wagon to safety around the corner.

"What's an orphan?" Henry had asked him.

"Nothin'," Harry had answered sharply." Just some stupid word they made up. Don't mean nothin'."

Henry had never forgotten the word.

And Nita had sure enough fussed at them for breaking the milk bottle.

From his perch in the tree, Henry watched a faded red wooden-sided cattle truck turn onto the highway at the same time a shiny black '39 Ford coupe turned off of it onto the road. But he couldn't see any Japs, which was what he was looking for.

Below, he could watch Mr. Bailey trimming the weeds near the house with his clippers. He was sorry they didn't have more grass in the yard so there'd be more for Mr. Bailey to do when he came. Lying on the tree branch, he watched Harry circle the yard in a wobbling arc, his intent blond head passing under the tree.

Henry had tried to ride the bike himself, but the bar kept him from reaching the pedals. Judging from the problems Harry was having, he figured reaching the pedals wasn't all there was to it.

At the sound of a car door, Henry sat up, and peered warily through the leaves. The shiny black coupe had stopped, but it wasn't a Jap. It was only Mr. Rigby, Mama's boss, heading up the driveway on short legs under his plump belly. He was the only man Henry knew who wore a suit and tie every time you saw him, even in summer. Today's suit was dark and pin-striped and his tie had an amazing chartreuse and gold hula girl painted on it above the word "Aloha." Even at this distance and angle, Henry could tell Mr. Rigby was sweating shinily under his wide snap-brimmed straw hat. Sourly eyeing Mr. Bailey, Mr. Rigby passed under the tree.

"If you was a Jap," Henry said from above, "I'd have to drop a coconut on your head."

Both of Mr. Rigby's short legs left the ground at the same time. He looked up, alarmed, toward Henry's bare feet.

"Hey, boy," he said angrily, "why is it you always up in that tree?"

"Watching the Japs," Henry answered proudly. "I'm doing it for Mr. Roosevelt. I do it every day." It was the most important thing he did these days.

"That's nonsense," Mr. Rigby snapped, straightening his hat.

Henry looked down at him incredulously. Nonsense?

14

"We *got* to watch for them," he said. "Lemme show you what they look like." Once again he wiggled himself into position, concentrated mightily, swung himself around the branch, and fell in a heap, rolling over in the dirt.

"Listen, Henry," said Mr. Rigby, slapping with his hat at the new dust on his pin-striped pants. "I don't have time for this foolishness."

Henry brushed off his overalls, hitched them up, and began digging in his back pocket. "I wanna show you what they *look* like," he insisted, pulling out a folded-up paper, a page torn from *Life* magazine.

"I know what they look like, for godsake," said Mr. Rigby, flicking with a chartreuse and gold handkerchief at the dust now on his hat.

Henry held out the black and white cartoon drawing, almost worn through from frequent foldings and unfoldings, of a barefooted Japanese soldier with a huge head, round steel-rimmed glasses, eyes like rifle-slits into the world of evil, and buck teeth bared in a demonic grin.

Mr. Rigby stared at it.

"Only they're yellow," Henry said.

"Why don't you plant a garden or something?" Mr. Rigby stuffed his handkerchief back into his pocket and replaced his hat on his balding head.

"Around here they drive submarines mostly," Henry added. "They come in at night from the Gulf."

"Henry, listen," said Mr. Rigby, lifting his left pants leg to put his foot on the step, "I got business. . . "

15

"They're short and they're mean," Henry interrupted, "and if you see one you come tell me and I'll go tell Mr. Roosevelt."

Mr. Rigby did not see Harry and the bicycle until they suddenly zigzagged past him, missing his pin-striped rear end by two or three inches. Both of his feet left the ground at the same time again.

"Hey, goddam boy!" he yelled when he landed. "Watch that fool thing, will you!"

The second that Harry looked fearfully back over his shoulder the bike wavered out of control and sent him sprawling in the dirt once more.

Shooting a baleful look at Mr. Rigby, Mr. Bailey limped toward Harry to help him up. The look caused Mr. Rigby to consider the use of several nearby objects as weapons of defense, including the rake, the upturned wagon, and the offending bicycle. Mr. Bailey's face in the best of moods was not a pretty sight, and angry, it caused Mr. Rigby's hula girl to bob up and down nervously under the knot at his throat.

"Your mama home?" he asked Henry quickly when the crippled handyman had turned his attention to Harry's scraped knee.

"Mama's *always* home," said Henry in the voice he used when adults insisted on acting like they were stupid or didn't know something he knew they did.

Mr. Rigby took another step up toward the porch, as Mr. Bailey glared toward him again, or rather half-glared, with the half of his forehead that could make a frown.

"Jesus," said Mr. Rigby to himself.

"Want another look?" Henry demanded, holding out the cartoon toward him.

Mr. Rigby made it to the top step, cast another apprehensive glance over his shoulder at Mr. Bailey, and reached for the front screen.

He could hear Nita at the switchboard in the middle room, placing an order, evidently, with that busybody Buford, the grocer.

". . . and I guess some baking soda . . . one box'll do. And a couple of oranges and maybe four or five potatoes . . . middle size. And . . . oh, a box of corn flakes. . . . I guess that's all. How much does that come to, Mr. Buford?"

Mr. Rigby stood in the doorway between the front and middle room. Jesus, but it was hot in this roachtrap.

Nita looked up at him coldly as he mopped his face with his handkerchief.

"And how many ration stamps?" she said into the mouthpiece.

Mr. Rigby returned her look and stuffed the damp cloth back into his pocket.

"All right," she said, reaching for the cord, "the boys'll be down in a minute . . . and thank *you*, Mr. Buford." She unplugged the cord and thrust a knife-like look toward Mr. Rigby as he cleared his throat.

"On company time . . ." he said, grateful that she had given him what he considered an appropriate opening remark for an employer.

"We have to eat," she replied, glancing at the hula girl.

Mr. Rigby looked behind him toward the door.

"You shouldn't let that ugly raggedy man hang around here," he said sourly.

"Mr. Bailey?" Nita's tone was overly polite.

"It's not good for business, somebody that looks like that. You ever seen him up close?"

"No, I haven't," Nita admitted, "but if looks were gold, Mr. Rigby . . ." She paused, letting the sentence trail off, surprised at the anger she was feeling toward him, surprised at how strong writing the letter had made her. "You wouldn't exactly be a rich man yourself," she had almost said to him. She smiled.

Coughing once, Mr. Rigby changed the subject but not the nature of his attack. "And that little boy of yours. We can't have him bothering everybody that walks in here. That's bad for business too, that boy sitting up in that tree like a damn idjit."

Nita looked at her knuckles, knotted white over the envelope on the table in front of her. When the switchboard buzzed and flashed its light, she lifted her eyes to meet Mr. Bailey's as she plugged in the cord to work the call.

"Number please," she said, not taking her eyes off her boss. "Thank you. I'll connect you." The letter would go in the mail today. No one could stop it.

"The receipts are in the drawer," she said to him, as she stood up and took off the headset. "Excuse me." She stepped past him to the front door, pushing open the screen.

"Harry!" she called. "Henry! Y'all take the wagon and go get the groceries. Here's the

18

money and the stamps." She held out a black coin purse. "And mail this," she added, licking the envelope to seal it.

Harry ran up the porch steps two at a time.

"Nita!" Mr. Rigby called from inside. "I don't see where Mr. Daniel Hooten paid this month."

"Henry! Be careful!" she cried, ignoring her boss, as her younger son tumbled into the dirt at the foot of the chinaberry. "One of these days you're gonna fall out of that tree and break your silly neck."

"Aw, Mama . . ." said Henry, hoisting his overalls with one hand and brushing them off with the other.

"We oughta disconnect him," Mr. Rigby called.

"He paid," she called back curtly. "It's there."

"Mama, can we get an Orange Crush at the store?" Henry asked, jumping from one foot to the other.

"No, baby," she said. "Not today. There's not enough money, maybe next time." It hurt having to say no to something so simple, so small. That was part of the reason for the letter. "Maybe next time," she repeated.

"Don't lose the letter or the money, Harry," she cautioned, as Henry turned the wagon over and climbed in, waiting for Harry.

"No, Mama," said Harry. "We won't."

"Okay, here it is," Mr. Rigby called back. "Gotta keep track of these things, you know. Can't have freeloaders, not in wartime."

Nita watched the boys out of the yard and across the road, Harry pulling and Henry riding, holding tightly onto the coin purse and her letter. It was out of her hands now. Gone, with a sigh of relief.

She glanced quickly at Mr. Bailey, now raking the bare dirt of the yard into little furrows. He had picked up all the toys and placed them neatly on the end of the porch. He did not look up.

When she turned back indoors, Mr. Rigby was sitting on the couch in the front room, still sorting through the receipts and bills. She walked straight past him into the middle room and sat down at the switchboard. She picked up her headset and took a deep breath.

"I think I should tell you, Mr. Rigby," she said, "I wrote a letter."

"How's that?" he responded absently, over the rustle of the papers. "You wrote a letter? Well, good for you!"

"I wrote a letter," Nita said evenly, "to try to get unfrozen from this job." She heard the papers stop rustling. "I wrote a judge," she finished.

"A judge?" cried Mr. Rigby with alarm. "Why'd you write some judge?"

At the buzz of the switchboard, she turned on her operator's voice, as thin and metallic as the wires that carried it, "Number please . . . thank you. I'll connect you."

Mr. Rigby was thinking it over. A judge? Sweat dripped from his chin onto the papers in his lap.

"If I don't look out for us, Mr. Rigby," she said with a tinge of anger that startled them both, "who will? You??"

Mr. Rigby considered his options.

"You know what'd make me friendlier . . ." he smiled suggestively, even though she couldn't see him. He waited for a reply.

There was none.

Mr. Rigby stopped smiling.

"Well," he said, crossing one option off his list, "maybe I can find you a better job within the company."

"That's what you been saying for two years," Nita replied doggedly.

He crossed off the second option.

"But Nita, a war's going on," he said with what he hoped was the voice of a tired administrator, harried almost beyond endurance by impossible employee demands. "Don't you know that?" he asked plaintively. "Nobody's on Easy Street these days."

"I ain't asking for Easy Street," Nita replied with a tremor in her voice. "I'm just asking for a chance to kiss my boys goodnight without being interrupted by a telephone switchboard!"

Mr. Rigby detected in her voice's quiver the tiniest crack in her assurance and knew he could escape through it.

"I can't help you," he said with authority. "I told you that. You're frozen in this job till the war's over or till the Texas Employment Agency says you're unfrozen."

"They'd change my status if you'd recommend it." Nita insisted, but her confidence was gone. She was asking him now, no longer telling him. It was over.

"I can't do that," said Mr. Rigby with finality.

"I'll just quit then!" Nita's voice rose with emotion. "I'll walk out!" she threatened shrilly.

"Go ahead," said Mr. Rigby, shaking his head. "But you won't get a job nowhere else, not if you violate the law of this country during its time of crisis and need!"

Nita's shoulders slumped. "You could help me if you would," she pleaded, "to get un-frozen . . ."

The buzzer cut through her hot frustration.

"Number please," she murmured automati-cally. "I'll connect you . . . I said I'll connect you!" She plugged in the cord and turned off the key.

Her hand fluttered nervously to the cross on the chain at her throat. What had happened to her confidence? She had felt so sure of her-self just a few minutes ago. She tried to imagine her letter dropping through the slot at the post office, lying next to a hundred other letters in the canvas mail bag, riding in the darkness to Corpus in the back of the blue and red truck. . .

"*Dear Judge*," he would read. "*Here is my situation . . .*"

Again she saw Francine's grief-stricken face in the air before her. She dropped her hand from her throat.

"*I know things are bad all over because of the war . . .*"

"I tell you what, Mr. Rigby," she said, her determination returning. "We're gonna get out of here. War or no war. Frozen or no frozen. And nobody like you is gonna keep us here." She paused. "You hear me?" she demanded.

There was no answer.

"Mr. Rigby?" she called.

She looked around the door into the front room. Mr. Rigby was no longer sitting on the couch. Mr. Rigby was nowhere in sight.

Nita pulled off the headset and walked to the front door in time to see the black Ford coupe with "Southwest Consolidated Telephone Company" painted on the door, driving down the road toward the highway.

Mr. Bailey, his work finished and his rake, hoe, and shovel reattached to the lawnmower, was clanking away across the yard.

Nita closed her eyes and leaned her head tiredly against the doorjamb.

"We can't go on living like this," she whispered into the warm wood. *"We can't go on . . ."*

4

Halfway down the block toward Buford's Grocery Store, Harry slowed the wagon and peered into the dusky interior of the seedy poolhall that stood between the feed store and the barbershop. Henry climbed out of the wagon and ducked his head under Harry's arm. Together they squinted into the darkness.

It was a routine they were both used to by now. Harry had explained to Henry what their mother had said, that the divorce had happened because their daddy had wanted to spend more time in the poolhalls drinking beer than at home with her and the boys. So Harry checked out the poolhall as often as possible, just to see if his dad had come back unannounced and headed straight for the place he'd rather be.

Harry wasn't sure how much of what he remembered about his daddy was real and how much was what he'd like to remember. Every once in a while he pulled the straight-back chair next to the radio and climbed up on it to look closely at the picture Mama kept on the whatnot shelf by the basket of china eggs she wouldn't let them play with. The picture was of his daddy and a little baby he knew was Henry and a little boy about three years old, holding his daddy's hand and grinning like a fool; that was Harry himself.

He thought he remembered that his daddy was bigger and stronger than anyone else he ever knew, that he smelled of tobacco and often of beer, that he had a loud voice when he and Mama argued late at night, and that his cheek was all bristly when he hugged you, not smooth like Mama's or like Harry's own.

Beyond that, he wasn't sure what he remembered. Had his daddy really taken him to a ranch near where they had lived, where they had ridden horses—or had Harry just wanted him to? Had they really built a train with wheels that turned, made out of tin cans and oatmeal boxes—or had Harry dreamed about it? Had his daddy really held him on his lap and told him stories about Indians living in the woods—or had Harry made up the stories himself?

When he had once asked Henry if he remembered the stories, the younger boy shook his head and eagerly asked to hear them.

Harry wished he could remember more.

Inside the poolhall, two naked light bulbs hung from the ceiling on twisted wires over the single pool table where two men were shooting a game of eight-ball. A long bar stretched across the wall behind the pool table, and behind the bar sat Crecencio Zamora, the Mexican bartender, surrounded by signs and posters: JAX BEER and R.C. COLA and KWITCHER-BELIAKEN and JOIN THE NAVY and Betty Grable and DR. PEPPER and BUY WAR BONDS and Rita Hayworth and CRECENCIO'S to match the neon outside the door.

"Pool shooters!" whispered Harry, as he carefully scrutinized the faces of the two men at the table.

"Yeah," Henry nodded. "Pool shooters."

The taller of the two pool shooters picked up his beer bottle off the bar and took a long swig.

"And beer drinkers!" said Harry, his eyes growing wide.

"Yeah," Henry agreed, "beer drinkers!"

The taller man, setting down his beer bottle, saw the two boys staring in the doorway and nudged his shorter, stupider-looking partner.

Now that Harry got a good look at them, they did not look a thing like his daddy. They looked, in fact, downright mean and ugly. He reached protectively for Henry's arm, as the taller pool shooter smiled nastily at the other and motioned toward the door.

"Sic 'em, Arnold," he whispered.

And, shouting and waving his arms crazily, the shorter one suddenly charged toward the boys. "Heah, you boys!" he cried, giggling maliciously. "Heah! Heah!"

Jerking Henry back from the doorway, Harry sprinted for the wagon handle. "Run!" he yelled. And together, the boys dashed down the cracked sidewalk past the barbershop, not daring to look back until they were in front of the grocery store's screen door with the "Come Again Rainbow Bread" handle.

Mr. Buford pushed open the door as the boys rattled and clanked to a stop. All three of them glared down the sidewalk toward the pool shooters who stood next to the faded red cattle truck, laughing and slapping their knees. The one called Arnold was pointing toward the boys, whooping.

"Pool shooters and beer drinkers!" said Harry disgustedly.

"Draft-dodging good-for-nothings!" said Mr. Buford as he ushered the boys into the store under his arm. He eyed the sign on the side of the truck: TRIPLETT BROTHERS, GENERAL HAULING, GREGORY, TEXAS.

The fat one was Arnold, who had, without much difficulty, convinced the members of the local draft board that he was too stupid to be trusted with a gun. The taller, meaner-looking one was his brother Calvin, who had, just as easily, convinced them that anyone too stupid to carry a gun and get shot by Japs was too stupid to be left roaming loose in Gregory all alone. So they let Calvin stay home to keep an eye on Arnold for them.

Sour and slime, Mr. Buford called them.

"What you boys been doing, anyway?" he asked, smiling at Harry and Henry as he set the two bags of groceries in the wagon.

"Oh, watching for Japs mostly," Henry answered, starting to dig in his pocket for the picture of the Japanese soldier.

Mr. Buford patted him on the head. "Showed

me that picture last week," he laughed, "remember?"

The grocer counted out the change and tokens and tore off the required stamps. "Okay, y'all be careful with that freight," he said, handing the purse back to Harry. "It's a pretty good load."

Henry had stuffed the picture back into his hip pocket, but he looked earnestly up at Mr. Buford. "They smile a lot," he said. "Sometimes you can tell them by that."

Mr. Buford nodded.

"And they're usually driving submarines," Henry continued.

"I'll keep an eye peeled," the grocer promised, as he reached under the counter for a small paper bag.

"Here's a little something special for you boys," he said, handing the bag to Henry, who excitedly untwisted the top.

"Oh boy!" cried Harry, peering in. "Jelly beans!"

"Hot diggity dog!" squealed Henry, reaching a fist into the sack and coming out with a dozen pieces of the candy.

Harry reached in. "Thanks, Mr. Buford."

"Yeah, thanks," said Henry, stuffing his mouth full.

"Now, y'all don't spill those groceries," Mr. Buford laughed, as the boys pulled the wagon through the front door.

Nice kids. And that poor woman, working night and day to feed them and buy them shoes for school and coats for the winter. 'Bout time she got them paid for one year, they'd outgrow them the next. Of course, he mused, as he watched the boys straighten out the wagon and start down the sidewalk, when a woman got divorced, she ought to expect some hardship. Shoulda thought more about that before she told her troubles to a judge. Better yet, she shoulda thought more about it before she ever married a man she didn't want to stay with and got herself them two kids. Divorcing her husband may have gotten rid of some of her troubles, but it sure had brought some others she probably hadn't counted on.

Outside, as Harry turned the wagon down the sidewalk, he saw the toes of two boots sticking out of the doorway to the poolhall. Above them protruded a beer belly, and, above that, the curled brim of a cowboy hat. He straightened the wheels and steadied the front sack of groceries with a hand as he eased the wagon carefully over the crack in the sidewalk.

Closer to the doorway, he could see there were two pairs of boots and two hat brims, though still only one beer belly. It belonged to the fat one called Arnold. The taller, skinnier, mean-looking man squinted at the approaching boys as he raised his beer bottle for a swallow. Harry kept his eyes on the groceries, hoping that if he didn't look at the men they wouldn't notice him.

But it didn't work. The taller one lowered his beer bottle as Harry passed and stuck his toe under the wagon's rear wheel. Henry grabbed at the swaying grocery bags as the wagon lurched to a standstill on the sidewalk. Harry jerked on the handle again.

"Where the hell you boys think you're goin' with them groceries?" Calvin asked.

"Home," Henry answered him. "Where do you think?"

Arnold began pawing through the grocery bags.

Harry jerked on the wagon tongue again, but Calvin still had his foot in the way.

"You better get outta that bag, Mister," Harry warned.

"Yeah?" sneered Arnold, pulling out an orange. "Looka here, Calvin," he said.

"Yeah!" Henry grabbed for the fruit.

"You're a smart little sonovabitch, ain't you?" Calvin laughed as Arnold jerked the orange away. "Want a beer?" he asked, offering his bottle.

"We're too young to drink beer!" Harry said quickly, tugging at the wagon again. "We gotta go home."

Arnold reached in for another orange. "Taking the groceries home to your mama, huh?" he said.

"I'd like to take the groceries home to your mama," Calvin leered, raising an eyebrow toward Arnold. They both laughed.

"Come on, Mister," Harry said, almost pleading. "We gotta go." He was afraid. None of this was funny. "Hey!" came the sharp yell from inside the poolhall.

All four of them turned to look.

"Hey, why don' ju peek on somebody jour own size?" Crecencio called from behind the bar.

"You shut up in there," Calvin yelled angrily, "or I'll clean your goddam Meskin plow!"

"Yeah," Arnold glowered. "Clean it!"

With an angry grunt, Crecencio pushed his bulk up from the cold box he was leaning against and started around the end of the bar. The customers. That was the only thing wrong with running a business like this. Everything else he liked fine: the pool table, the beer, the neon sign spelling out his name above the door. But the people, the customers, made him hate it—the drunks, the deadbeats, the down-and-outers. Especially these two, nothing but trouble. Sometimes he figured he just oughta sell the place and take that job driving the Lone Star truck they'd offered him more than once. . . .

As he passed the pool table, Crecencio picked up a cue and slapped the heavy butt end of it into his hand, imagining the satisfying crack it would make when he swung it as hard as he could against Calvin or Arnold's head—he didn't care which—maybe both. Picking on little kids.

As Crecencio reached for the screen, planning to come out swinging, Harry jerked the wagon once more, harder than before, pulling the back wheel over Calvin's boot. The grocery bags bounced and swayed and two potatoes fell out.

"Come on, Henry!" Harry chased a potato into the gutter.

"Why'd you do that?" Henry demanded, staring up belligerently at the pool shooters.

"You better git on with your brother, squirt," Calvin laughed, taking another swig of his beer. "Or I might take a mind to paddle your behiney."

Crecencio stood silently, just inside the doorway, balancing the pool cue in his hand. With their backs to him, he could take them both before they knew what was happening.

"Why ain't y'all off fighting the Japs?" Henry asked fiercely.

Calvin giggled.

Calvin lowered his beer bottle.

"Henry!" pleaded Harry, a few steps down the sidewalk with the wagon. "Come on!"

"You better git, you little monkey!" Calvin glared.

Henry clamped his hands on his hips and thrust out a defiant lower lip.

As Arnold made a quick grab for him, Henry dodged away, stopping just out of range.

"I hope the Japs get y'all!" he yelled, and ran to catch up with Harry.

Arnold grinned and nodded like the idiot he was, but Calvin frowned after them, taking another slow swig of beer as the wagon bumped along the rough pavement and Harry glanced back over his shoulder, worried.

Shit, thought Crecencio. No fight. He watched a moment longer and then turned back inside and laid the cue on the table. He noticed that Betty Grable, smiling at him from behind the bar, needed straightening.

On sudden impulse he pushed the heavy wooden door shut and locked it.

"Hey!" one of the Triplett brothers yelled.

Crecencio smiled back at Betty. This afternoon it would be just the two of them—no surly drunken customers, no unintelligible conversations, no arguments or fights. Just him and Betty Grable—with Rita Hayworth kibitzing from the sidelines.

"Hey, pepperbelly!" yelled Calvin from outside. "Open up!" He banged on the door.

"We're closed!" Crecencio yelled back. He tugged on the corner of Betty's picture and winked at her.

The boys lifted the wagon off the curb at the end of the block.

Harry glanced back once more, but the pool shooters had lost interest in them and had turned to kick viciously at the door of the bar.

"Listen," he said carefully, looking at his little brother, "don't tell Mama about those guys, Okay?"

Henry looked up from the groceries, his round face puzzled. "Okay," he nodded, then, "Why not?" he asked.

"Just 'cause," said Harry, reaching for the wagon handle.

There was something in his voice that kept Henry from asking anything else.

5

"Number please . . ."

Harry lay in bed that night staring by the dim light from the middle room at the horse-shaped water stain on the ceiling. His mother was repeating the words he'd heard her say at least a thousand times before.

"Thank you. I'll connect you . . ."

Though the night was warm, he pulled the damp sheet over him.

The horse looked like it was rearing on a big rock.

He wondered again which one was meaner: the fat one with the idiot laugh or the thin one with the squinty eyes. Arnold or Calvin. They were both horrible! He wished there were someone he could talk to about them.

There were so many things Harry didn't understand these days. Like why there was a war and why God had made Japs and Germans so mean and why his daddy had never come to see them and why his mother never laughed any more. Things he didn't understand made him feel afraid.

He turned over to see if Henry was awake, but the younger boy was sleeping soundly, his bedclothes on the floor beside the comic book he'd abandoned at bedtime.

Harry had felt the crawly feet of his fear earlier that night when it was time to go to the privy before bed. Having peeled off his overalls and unlatched the back door, he had stood in his jockey shorts for a long apprehensive moment in the doorway, flicking the flashlight's beam into every corner of the back yard. He couldn't have said exactly what he thought might be hiding out there, but whatever it was, he wanted to see it first.

He had been grateful when Henry had jumped up from his comic, crying, "Wait for me!" as he dropped his overalls and ran bareassed to the chest of drawers for a pair of jockey shorts to pull on. Harry was glad he didn't have to go alone into the closed-in darkness of the privy that night.

Inside the outhouse, they both peered into the black hole.

"Don't see any spider webs," Henry reported.

"Better make sure," Harry cautioned, pointing the flashlight at the stick they kept in the corner for this purpose.

Henry picked it up and ran it around and around inside the wooden hole.

"I guess it's Okay," Harry concluded, as they

both examined the stick for evidence of the dreaded black widows whose preference for privies was well known.

Henry looked into the darkness of the hole once more. "You go first," he said.

Back outside, Harry had once again cast the flashlight beam in all directions before they dashed for the back door.

"What are you looking for?" Henry had asked. "Why are we running?"

"Nothin' " Harry had whispered when they reached the back door. "Just running." He really didn't know the answers, but the un-named fear clawed at his insides.

He had latched the back door carefully against the two-legged, four-legged, thousand-legged night beasts that lurked beyond it and had listened for a moment for any noise, rat-tling of the doorknob or scratching at the crack above the doorsill.

Then he had walked quickly through the middle room, past his mother seated at the switchboard with her headset on, and into the darkened front room. There, on the little corner shelf over the radio, stood the picture in its tin frame and next to it the delicate white china basket with its smooth shiny eggs that Mama loved so much.

He pulled the chair over from the pay phone and lifted the picture down. Holding it close in the semi-darkness, he gazed intently into the man's crinkly eyes for some sign, some hint. . . .

Looking at the picture always made him feel better. He stood the frame back on the shelf and carefully picked up the white basket by its thin hard handle. In the dim light he could just make out the colors of the eggs: blue with white flowers painted on it, yellow with swirls of orange, pink and red, green with a blue-green bunny rabbit.

He turned the eggs over in his hand: smoother and hard and cool, like clear water would feel if it came in hard droplets. . . .

"Harry!" his mother had called from the middle room. "Are you in there? Time for bed."

In his room, Harry turned over in the narrow bed and said goodnight to the ceiling horse.

"Number please," he heard Nita repeat tiredly into her headset.

Harry closed his eyes.

"Just a moment, please. I'll connect you," was the last thing he heard as he rode the rearing horse into a troubled dream.

His daddy stood beside a tank just like the one on the sign outside the post office, wearing a uniform just like the one in the sign, with medals and ribbons all over his chest.

"Wait for me, Daddy!" Harry cried, but when he tried to run with him, his legs wouldn't work right and his feet seemed to bog down in the dirt.

His father spoke, but his words were lost in the firing of the guns from the tank. His mouth was moving but all Harry could hear was the *boom-boom* of the guns that exploded in bright-colored flowers like fireworks over his daddy's head.

When Harry started to cry, his daddy smiled softly and unpinned one of the medals from his jacket and held it out to the boy. He said something again, but all Harry could hear was the *boom-boom-boom* of the flowery exploding guns. And then his daddy climbed into the back and was gone.

Daddy! When Harry turned the medal over in his hand, he could see it was all red and gold with scrolly writing on it. Closing his fingers around it, he felt it warm and smooth.

6

Nita pulled off the headset and ran her fingers tiredly through the damp hair at the nape of her neck. She pulled the lace-edged neck of her gown away from the sweat that was trickling between her breasts. So hot, so late at night.

As she stepped out onto the porch, heat-lightning flared sullenly beyond the flattened horizon. Maybe it would rain. She sat on the step, leaning against the 2 x 4 post, and watched the silent electric display, like a distant flashing marquee or searchlights announcing the opening night of a world premiere, far off, somewhere else, for someone she could never know.

Between the lazy flares of lightning, Nita could see the stars glistening like the faceted beads on the black satin dress that hung in her closet.

"I'll make a wish upon a sta-a-ar . . ." she hummed.

She'd bought the dress on layaway, to go dancing with Walter. Took her six, maybe eight months to pay for it and get it out. Now it hung limply in the dark under a slit-open paper bag to keep the dust off, its beads reflecting no glisten at all.

". . . and wake up where the clouds are far be-hind me . . ."

The lightning blazed again, noiselessly, glittering through its low-hung cloudbank.

Nita sighed and fanned the gown about her legs, gazing across the road, beyond the vacant lot where the cow grazed, toward town, where the porch and window lights of the separate houses converged under the red beacon on top of the water tank and the white neon cross above the Methodist church. She knew that on the other side of the cluster, the lights thinned out again into the coastal darkness, beyond which the soft lightning illuminated the far-off clouds over the black-watered Gulf. A mosquito buzzed near her ear.

In the center of the cluster of lights at this moment a beer bottle spun across the sidewalk and slammed against the closing door of the pool hall, splintering the warm night under the red neon letters: CRECENCIO'S.

"Look up there, Pancho Villa!" Calvin giggled down the empty street, echoing the bottle he had flung.

"Closing time," came the bartender's voice from within.

The door locked from inside and the neon

40

sign went out, leaving the Triplett brothers leaning drunkenly against the fender of their trunk.

"Shit. Let's go," Arnold mumbled.

Nita slapped at a mosquito which landed on her arm, just as the truck turned off the highway and started down the road toward her house, past Francine's. She stood up, glancing at the approaching lights as she pulled open the screen and stepped inside from the dark porch.

"Hey, by God, how do you like that, Arnold?" Calvin cried, slowing the truck to get a better look at the woman's long legs and full breasts silhouetted starkly through the thin gown.

"I like that just fine," his brother giggled, craning back over his shoulder.

Nita closed the door and turned off the front room light.

"Maybe we'll just fix you up one of these nights, little brother," Calvin laughed, and clamped his foot on the accelerator.

7

When the rain moved in a few hours later, gently at first, patting the dry leaves of the chinaberry tree with soft fingers, and then turning the raked furrows of the yard into stippled mud, Nita was fast asleep. She didn't wake even when the tap of the drops on the tin roof became a steady hammering and the thunder rattled the unputtied glass in the lightning-lit windows.

It was the raucous voice of the switchboard that yanked her suddenly wide awake, tight-nerved and blinking into its own winking eye. Oh yes. She pushed herself off the cot and reached for the headset.

"Number please . . ." she said sleepily, plugging in the cord and turning on the key without even sitting down. A brilliant flash of lightning threw the black paper cutout of her shadow across the desk and the wall.

At the moment the lightning flared, a casual

glance into the wet brush of the vacant lot across the road would have shown Nita a figure, another flat black shadow outlined by the sudden blaze of light, a real figure, not the cat she had imagined or unnamed demons Harry had feared—but a man half-concealed behind the roadside mesquite, hunkered against the rain, silent, unmoving, intent upon her window and her barely visible shape at the switchboard in the darkened room.

But Nita hadn't looked.

"Just a moment, please. I'll connect you," she yawned, as the thunder crashed and roared and the dishes clattered together in the cabinet.

After she disconnected the call, she looked in on the sleeping boys—Harry, the sheet pulled up to his neck, and Henry, with no sheet at all.

It must be hard for them, she thought—nobody to take them any place, not even any other kids to play with, and her with barely enough energy to get their meals on the table and not even enough money to buy them an Orange Crush. Henry was still the open-faced little kid he'd always been. But Harry—she worried about Harry. He kept so much inside.

She could hear the rain battering the upturned wagon in the yard. At least maybe it'd cool things off for a little while.

A few minutes after she lay back down on the cot, she was sound asleep again.

It wasn't the scream of the switchboard that woke her the second time, an hour or so later. It was a knock on the front door, quiet at first, and then, when there was no response, louder, insistent.

43

Nita struggled back to consciousness again, pushing aside the rain's noise, listening for the switchboard, trying to figure what had wakened her.

The knock came again, louder still, a banging.

Fully awake now, she sat up and pulled on her old blue robe.

At the front door she switched on the porch light, turning the nearest raindrops into a shimmering scrim, and opened the door a crack, keeping the chain lock on.

Dripping wet in his white uniform, a young sailor stood there, smiling hopefully at her. He pulled his cap off his close-cropped blond hair.

"Yes?" said Nita.

"I'm sorry," he stammered. "I really am. But I need to phone. . ." He shook his head unhappily. "I'm sorry to bother you like this. Man at the gas station said you had a pay phone. . . . "

Back lit by a brilliant flash, his face turned dark as the yard blazed brightly enough to see colors there—red of the boys' wagon, blue of the old bike.

"It's Okay," Nita shrugged sleepily, pushing the door far enough to release the chain. "Come on in."

It was nothing new, being jerked awake like this by someone banging against her door—frantically or fearfully or just purposefully, stubbornly, persistently. It was part of her job —apologetic Jean Lester trying to get a line through while it was daytime *over there*, to tell Jack, her husband, that the new baby had

44

come; Mrs. Buford, red-eyed and exhausted in her grief from being up two nights with her bed-ridden, failing mother, calling her sister in Fort Worth to say that the old lady had finally, mercifully, died and that they'd better all come tomorrow for the laying-out; the terrified father begging in half-English, half-Spanish for the doctor please to treat his son, seven years old and bit by a six-foot rattler, *por favor*, while the injured boy and his siblings and mother wailed into the scaly-eyed darkness from the old Chevy parked on the road. Holy Mary, Mother of God.

Each one different, another story, another happiness or fear or grief, pulled to Nita's front room by the strand of telephone wire that ran from the switchboard to the pole beside the road. Out of the darkness, drawn like moths to the blinking eye of the switchboard, banging on her door in the middle of the night with something they had to say to someone else that couldn't wait for morning.

And then they were gone—the excited wife, the exhausted and grieving daughter, the pleading father, and soon this young sailor too; gone, with barely a memory that they had dragged a tired-looking blonde-haired woman wrapped in a blue bathrobe out of bed in the middle of the night to plug in the wires of the switchboard and say, "Number please . . ."

And Nita would lie down on her cot in the switchboard's lair and wait for the next one. There would always be a next one, like tonight, like this young sailor here, dripping on her porch from the rain.

"I'm gonna get your floor all wet," he said apologetically, stamping his feet before he came in. He was awful young, maybe nineteen or twenty.

"It's Okay," she said, tiredly. "Don't worry about it. I'm used to it."

"I'm sorry," he said, dropping his wet sea bag by the door.

Nita shook her head. "There's the pay phone," she motioned toward the wall between the front room and the middle room. "You got change?"

"Yes, ma'am," he nodded, jamming a hand into his pocket like a kid.

Stepping past him into the middle room, Nita pulled the door to the front closed behind her and turned to the switchboard on the other side of the wall.

"Number please," she said into the headset.

"Oh!" The sailor sounded surprised. "That you, lady?" He said it into the receiver, but she could hear him through the thin wall as well.

"Sorry," said Nita. "Habit."

"Let's see . . ." he said. "Number one-eight-two. Stillwater, Oklahoma."

Nita reached for the cord. "Person or station?" she asked.

"Ma'am?"

"Person-to-person or station-to-station?" Nita repeated automatically,.

He hesitated.

"Station's cheaper," she offered.

"Station," he answered quickly.

Nita turned on the key. "Operator, this is Gregory," she began in her monotone. "MX to Stillwater, Oklahoma . . . number one-eight-two . . . my party is holding." She could do it in her sleep, she was sure. She was almost doing it that way now.

"It'll take a minute," she said to the sailor. "Deposit fifty-five cents for the first three minutes when they answer."

"Yes, ma'am," came the sailor's excited voice through both the headset and the wall. "I'll wait."

They both listened to the clicks, the buzzes, the operators' voices, and the hums as the call worked its way from her switchboard under the rain-struck roof, to Corpus, to Dallas, to Oklahoma City, and finally to Stillwater. Nita closed her eyes and waited. She could almost hear the sailor's breathless anticipation on the other side of the wall.

"They're ringing now," she told him when she heard the familiar sound.

"Maybe nobody's home," he sighed after a few seconds.

"It's still ringing."

"Gosh, I wish she'd answer," she heard him whisper.

Must be calling his girl. Nita sighed. Everybody going someplace. Everybody calling someone.

A sleepy hello cut through the lines.

Nita heard the sailor gulp and listened as the coins clinked dully into the machine. Two quarters and a nickel.

"Mrs. Shinn?" he said eagerly.

Nita switched off her key.

"Mrs. Shinn? Hello!" She could hear him just

as clearly through the wall. "This is Teddy! Teddy! . . . I'm calling from Texas. . . . "

Nita closed her eyes again.

"Yes, ma'am, 'Deep in the He-a-a-a-rt of Tex-as!'" he sang. "Some state, what I've seen of it. . ."

Nita smiled.

"Yes, ma'am, I am . . . I sure am fine. How are all y'all? Oh, that's good. I'm glad. That's real good . . ."

Nita was listening to the rain, the wind among the leaves of the chinaberry, the rumble of the far-away thunder.

"Listen, Mrs. Shinn, can I talk to Charlotte? I know it's late, and I'm sorry, but I'm hitch-hiking in from Texas. I wanna tell her I'm on the way. . . . "

Going home to see his girl. Going off to war, like Emile Lucas, like Jack Lester, like Walter. . . . Nita was almost dreaming.

"Yes, ma'am, tonight," she heard him say. "I got a five-day leave . . . no, ma'am, that's not long. It's sure not. But I'm on my way . . . ma'am?"

Some slight change in his tone made Nita open her eyes.

"Well, why not, Mrs. Shinn?" he asked.

"Ma'am?" he said, a hint of surprise coming through the wall, maybe even of alarm. "Ma'am?" he repeated with definite alarm.

Nita caught her breath.

"When was that, Mrs. Shinn?" he asked, shocked.

"Mrs. Shinn, are you teasing me?" he said suddenly.

"No, ma'am," he acknowledged. "No, ma'am. I guess you wouldn't. . . .

"Yes, ma'am," he said then, with resignation. "Well, I appreciate that. I always liked you and Mr. Shinn, too. . . .

"Who to, Mrs. Shinn?" he asked.

"Him?" His voice was flat. "Really? . . ."

"No, ma'am, just kinda surprised, that's all . . . yes, ma'am. He's a mechanic, ain't he? At Willis Chevrolet?"

Under the tiny light on top of the switchboard, Nita rubbed her hand across her eyes.

"Yes, ma'am, I know him . . . well, I didn't know him that well, Mrs. Shinn, but I'm sure he is." She could tell he wanted to stop talking, stop hearing.

"Well, listen, Mrs. Shinn . . . I better go. . . . No, ma'am, just kinda caught me off guard, I guess. . . . Yes, ma'am, I will. Yes, ma'am. . . . And Mrs. Shinn . . . would you tell Charlotte . . ."

His voice trailed off. "Tell Charlotte . . . well, I don't know . . . goodbye, I guess . . . I'm gonna miss her, Mrs. Shinn. . . . "

There was a pause.

"Oh, no, ma'am, nothing ever bothers me for long," he said then, too friendly, too hearty. "Well, you tell Mr. Shinn hello for me, too . . . Okay . . ."

Nita felt the weight of it pushing her down into the chair. So young, like a kid. . . .

"I will. Thank you," he said. "Yes ma'am. Okay . . ." his voice trailed off again, weak, like a piece of twine unraveling. "Bye-bye, Mrs. Shinn. . . . "

Nita waited for him to hang up, but he didn't.

She turned her key.

"All through?" she said sadly into the headset.

"She married Jimmy Tompkins," the sailor responded into the phone.

"Oh . . . Nita murmured apologetically.

"Yeah . . . that was sure a surprise to me," he said.

"I guess it was," Nita nodded. "I'm sorry. . . ."

"Oh, I'll get over it," he offered bravely.

She felt almost as if she had said it to him: You'll get over it, son.

"I know. . . ." she responded.

"But it sure does surprise the heck outta me right now," he repeated, drawing a long breath. "She's a fine lady, Charlotte. We was . . . talking about getting married ourselves. . . . I never even thought about it with anybody else. Pretty, you know, and sweet . . ."

"You want some coffee?" Nita asked gently.

"Thanks," he sighed, "but I guess I better hitch on back to the base in Corpus."

"It'll make you feel better. . . ."

There was a long pause.

"Well," he said sadly, "I kinda doubt it, ma'am. . . . It musta been the getting married she liked more than me. Jimmy Tompkins . . ."

Nita listened to the rain on the roof.

"I'm gonna have a cup," she said, as a clap of thunder shook the dishes and the window panes. "Sure you don't want one?"

"Well," he sighed, "Okay. Might as well, I guess."

Nita turned off her key and unplugged the cord. She pushed open the door to the front room.

"In here," she smiled at the top of his blond, short-cropped head bent over his elbows on his knees.

The kitchen was really just the other side of the middle room, opposite the switchboard and the cot. Nita put the coffee pot on the fire to warm and reached two cups down off their hooks. With the dish rag she wiped off the metal card table.

He stepped through the door from the front room.

"Those your boys?" he asked, nodding toward the back room.

"Yeah," Nita smiled, "Henry and Harry. Henry's the little one."

"I got a little brother." He stood awkwardly in the middle of the room.

"Really?"

"Yes, ma'am," he nodded. "His name's Ronnie. Wanted to join the Navy with me."

"Too young, huh?" Nita smiled as she poured the coffee.

"Yes, ma'am." He grinned and leaned against the wall. "He's only five."

Nita set the two cups of coffee on the card table and opened the refrigerator. "Cream?"

"Yes, ma'am, please."

She set the bottle of milk on the table. "Why don't you sit down?" she asked, smiling.

He grinned, still embarrassed, and pulled out a chair.

"Sugar?" she asked, reaching up on the high shelf over the sink where she kept the bowl.

"Aw, I wouldn't want to take any of your sugar." He shook his head as he poured off some of the cream that had risen into the neck of the milk bottle.

"It's Okay," Nita smiled. "I don't get a chance to bake very much."

"Well," said the sailor.

She set the bowl in front of him.

"I have to keep it up high," she laughed, "or Henry'll eat it by the handful." She sat down and picked up her coffee cup.

It was a minute before she realized that he was still putting spoonfuls of sugar into his cup and that the coffee was running over into the saucer.

"Oh," he laughed, embarrassed. "Look at me!"

Nita smiled and took a sip of her coffee, but she couldn't think of anything to say. Poor kid.

A flash of lightning lit up the rainy world outside the window.

"It must hurt," she finally said, motherly, as if he had bumped his head or scraped his knee.

He tried to smile, shaking his head. "I didn't think this kinda thing happened till you got overseas."

Nita laughed sympathetically.

"I mean, I thought . . . " he frowned and continued to stir his coffee. "I thought if we really cared about each other, nothing bad could happen. . . . "

"There's always bad things can happen," Nita said softly.

He nodded, still staring at the cup.

52

"Maybe she got scared," Nita said gently. "Scared about the war."

He looked up.

"Scared you wouldn't come back, maybe. Scared something bad could happen."

He took a sip of coffee and then set the cup down and rubbed his eyes.

"Yeah," he said tiredly. "Scared. Like I'm scared. Maybe that's why I wanted to see her so bad again . . . before we shipped out. . . . "

It was everywhere, the war. No one escaped. If Nita listened closely, she could hear it right now, sloshing through the ditch water into her muddy yard. Closer and closer . . .

"There's nothing to do but go on. . . . " she said finally, looking down.

"I'll get over it," he said softly, trying to convince himself.

Nita nodded.

"Is that too sweet?" She noticed his grimace as he took a swallow of the coffee. "I can pour you some more."

"Oh, no," he shook his head manfully as he drained his cup. "Just the way I like it."

He pushed his chair back. "I guess I better go."

Nita followed him to the front door.

"I appreciate the coffee."

"That's all right," she smiled.

He cast a last look at the pay phone on the opposite wall and, picking up his sea bag, pulled open the door.

When the lightning flashed, Nita could see that the once carefully raked yard was now a sea of water and mud rising toward the porch.

A clap of thunder exploded like a shell over their heads and the bombardment of the rain grew heavier.

The sailor extended his hand to her. "Thanks," he said, a little awkwardly, "you know . . . for everything. . . ."

Shaking his hand, Nita looked at him apprehensively.

"Listen," she said hesitantly, "you can stay here tonight. . . ." It wasn't only that she was worried about him out there. She was also worried about herself in here tonight . . . and the boys . . . if he left. . . .

"Oh, no," he said quickly. "I better get on."

"But it's so messy out there. Nobody'll be on the road. You'll never get a ride. . . ." She was almost pleading.

He turned and looked off in the torrent.

"Well . . ."

"It's Okay. You can sleep in here on the couch in the front room. . . ."

He turned back toward her.

"I didn't mean for you to have to adopt me," he smiled sheepishly.

"I'll get you a couple of sheets," said Nita, relieved, and pushed the door to.

As her mind slipped down the rain-slick incline toward sleep, Nita turned on her cot and dreamed first that it was Emile Lucas knocking on her door in the middle of the night to make a phone call to his mother. *"But you're . . ."* she faltered, not quite able to tell him he was dead. He had smiled sadly at her. And then it was Harry, his blond hair wet from the storm, knocking on Francine's door, crying *"Mama!"*

and Francine throwing the door open, to grab Harry to her bosom and cry, *"Emile! My son!"* And then it was the young sailor crying *"Charlotte! Charlotte!"* And then it was Walter looking at Nita blankly and not saying a word. . . .

When the lightning flashed across her cot, across her closed eyelids, Nita moaned uneasily but slept on, unaware of its flare of light.

The sailor on the maroon couch in the front room opened his eyes for a moment into the dazzling glare, and then closed them again, to let the steady drone of the rain wash his troubled mind clean. Nothing to do but go on . . .

At the edge of the vacant lot across the road, however, the dark figure of the man that had huddled there earlier still crouched, staring over the suddenly lighted and then darkened rainscape toward the house, steadily, relentlessly, reptilian in his waiting, his gaze eternal, sleepless, round and pale and lidless.

8

Harry was surprised to find the door between the middle room and the front room closed in the morning light, but he and Henry were halfway through the front room before he saw the reason why.

"What's that?" Henry gasped, freezing in his tracks and pointing at the white lump on the maroon couch, "A Jap?"

"Shhh!" Harry whispered. "I don't know!"

"I better get my gun!" Henry tiptoed back through the middle room. A Jap at last!

Harry took a step closer to the couch, peering at the sleeping face. It didn't look at all yellow.

"Daddy?" he whispered tentatively.

"Reach for the sky!" Henry bellowed, jamming the end of his old wooden rifle under the ear of the sleeping sailor.

The blue eyes popped open, wide and round. They weren't the least bit slanted.

"Reach, or I'll blow you to kingdom come!" Henry snarled.

The sailor swallowed and blinked at Harry and Henry.

"Who are you?" Harry asked curiously. It wasn't Daddy and he didn't think it was a Jap.

"What do you think you're doing on our couch?" Henry demanded.

The sailor grinned and stuck his hands up over his head. "Look," he said, "I don't want any trouble. I'm just passing through town."

"Hey!" cried Harry, catching sight of the Navy collar and tie. "You're a sailor!"

"You better keep those hands up!" Henry threatened, when the sailor smiled at Harry.

Harry smiled back.

"He's one of ours, Henry," he said, laying a hand on the wooden rifle barrel. "He's not a Jap. You can put your gun down."

"You gonna fight the Japs?" Henry asked, wide-eyed, lowering the gun.

"I guess I am," the sailor nodded. He sat up and straightened his tie and ran a hand over his short-cropped hair.

"Boy!" said Henry, too impressed to be disappointed that he hadn't caught a Jap after all.

The metallic growl of the switchboard cut through the morning air.

"Number please . . . " they heard Nita say sleepily in the middle room.

"You wanna come out and play with us?" Henry asked, poking the sailor.

"I wish I could," he smiled. "But I got to be getting on back to the base." He squatted down beside his sea bag.

"Why?" Harry asked, watching him tie the cord. "You shipping out?"

The sailor looked up. "In a few days," he said kindly.

Henry poked at the sea bag with his toy gun. "You might git kilt," he observed excitedly, "by the Japs."

"I'll be careful," the sailor smiled, patting him on the head.

"Boys!" Nita called urgently from the middle room. "Phone call for Mrs. Lester!" She appeared in the doorway in her blue chenille robe. "Hurry! Hurry now!"

Harry ran to the front door. "Wait here!" he cried to the sailor as he flung himself out on the porch, with Henry right behind him.

"Good morning." The sailor smiled up at Nita, but she had turned back to her switchboard.

"I'll have your party in a moment," she said in a worried tone into the headset. "Please hold the line."

She went back to the front door.

"I hope it's . . . nothing . . . too bad," she said softly to herself more than to the sailor, as she looked down the street.

Once again Francine Lucas's tormented face rose up before her eyes. No, thought Nita, no. Those cool, crisp military voices always rustled with the same dry papery stiffness, as if the same government-issue memo were circulating in quintuplicate in military mouths all over the country. It chilled her blood now to hear one asking for Jean Lester.

When she saw Jean's door fly open and the

woman flash toward the road, flanked by Harry and Henry, Nita ran to the switchboard.

"She's coming!" she said breathlessly into the headset before running back to the door. "Hurry, Jean!" she called.

The sailor stood up as he heard the other woman running across the yard and up the steps. But he wasn't quite sure what the worry and urgency were all about.

Jean Lester yanked the door open and stood as if rooted in the doorway, a baby in her arms, her eyes searching his face desperately.

"Is it Jack?" she asked.

"Ma'am," he stammered, "I . . . "

"They're on the line, Jean," Nita called anxiously from the middle room. "It's . . . Washington, D.C. . . . " she added.

Jean Lester took two steps toward the pay phone on the wall and stopped. "Nita?" she said fearfully.

"I don't know . . . " Nita answered her unspoken question. She stood in the doorway, helplessly fingering the cross at her throat.

Jean shifted the baby to one arm and reached for the receiver, her eyes unseeing. "Hello . . . " she whispered, trembling. "Yes it is," she said, covering her quivering mouth with her hand.

Nita stepped quickly to her side and held her tightly, as if to help brace against the dreaded news, the other woman's small body and the even smaller one she held.

"Jack's been shot!" she sobbed.

"Yes . . . yes . . . " she cried into the phone.

"But he's alive!" she gasped to Nita through her tears.

"Yes, I understand," Jean said into the phone. "Yes, I will."

Nita hugged her tightly.

"Yes, I appreciate it," said Jean. "Thank you. Yes. Goodbye." She hung up the phone and collapsed into sobs.

The baby began to cry.

"He's coming home," Jean gasped.

Nita's tears were falling in Jean's dark hair.

"Thank God, Jean," she whispered.

"Yes," Jean nodded tearfully. "Thanks, Nita." She hugged the baby to her bosom, but it was still wailing.

Together they walked to the door.

"Thank you," Jean cried to the sailor, throwing an arm around his neck in a tearful embrace. "Oh, thank you!"

"Oh," said the sailor, not quite sure how to respond. "Oh, sure . . . " He patted her awkwardly on the back.

Jean pushed open the screen.

"Jack's alive and he's coming home!" she cried to Harry and Henry as they ran across the yard toward the porch.

"Did he shoot any Japs?" Henry asked, but Mrs. Lester was beyond hearing, beyond caring, as she raced toward home with her precious news.

Wiping her eyes, Nita smiled at the sailor.

"I guess I'll be going now," he said, shouldering his sea bag. "Thanks for letting me stay last night."

"That's Okay," Nita smiled. "I'm glad you did. That was some rain!"

At the buzz of the switchboard, she shook

her head, smiled, raised a hand in farewell, and disappeared through the middle room doorway.

Harry bounded up the steps onto the porch.

"You ready now?" he asked through the screen.

"Ready? Ready for what?" the sailor responded, grinning as he stepped out the door with his sea bag.

"Well," Henry answered, exasperated, hands on his hips, "you're a *sailor,* ain't you?"

9

Under a full head of steam, the huge ship leaned into the sun-sparkled waves and plowed toward the open sea. Without warning, a dark shadow of foreboding fell across the boy.

Teddy looked up from the rain-filled ditch to the pair of broken shoes and the faded overalls towering over them.

"Mr. Bailey!" Henry cried excitedly. "Hi!"

"Look what we got!" Harry lifted the rubber-band-propelled paddlewheel boat out of the water.

"Teddy made it!" Henry grinned, pointing at the sailor.

Teddy felt himself caught and probed by the squinted eye. Apprehensively, he got to his feet.

But Mr. Bailey only nodded and squatted down beside the boys to watch Henry rewind the boat's wheel. Teddy relaxed and smiled as the little craft floated slowly across the muddy ditch, and Henry giggled, clapping his hands.

After a minute, Mr. Bailey pulled himself to his feet again, casting his crooked shadow once more over their inland sea.

"Got to go, Mr. Bailey?" Harry asked.

The handyman nodded and turned toward Teddy with a peculiar look. There was a strange approval in his half-smile, but there was something else, too—was it a sizing-up? A challenge? A threat?

Teddy smiled back, unsure, embarrassed before the silent man.

"Bye, Mr. Bailey," Henry called, winding up the boat again.

Mr. Bailey shuffled off.

Uncomfortable now, Teddy squatted down by the boys. What had that look meant? Not knowing made him uneasy. After another minute of watching the paddlewheel run into the weeds, he glanced at the sun. With any luck hitching, he could be back at the base in a couple of hours at the most.

"Boys," he said, "I'm gonna have to go too . . . really."

"But Teddy!" There was anguish in Harry's voice. "What about the kites?"

"What?" he said, surprised.

"Kites!" said Henry. "Don't you know how to make a kite?"

Teddy pushed his hat back and scratched his head, looking from one small pleading blond face to the other. "Kites . . ." he murmured.

Nita was watching from the front door as the three of them chopped sticks from the brush in the vacant lot and then squatted in the dust under the chinaberry tree, their blond heads bending close together as they cut the flattened grocery bags with her sewing scissors and glued the pieces to the sticks with the flour-and-water paste she'd mixed up for them.

He was a nice kid, to spend time with two little boys, and him with trouble of his own.

From the middle room as she was slicing the Spam for supper, she heard a whoop and a chorus of giggles.

"Give it a pull!" Teddy hollered, followed by more giggles and Harry shouting, "I am! I am!"

She got to the screen door in time to see her older son dashing headlong through the brush, watched by the idly chewing cow, as the fatally stricken kite swooped in menacing circles ever closer to the ground.

"Watch out, cow!" yelled Henry, and Nita heard herself laugh out loud as the kite, in its swan swoop, landed in the alarmed beast's horns, flapping its tail wildly about her ears. Laugh out loud—it almost seemed unnatural, but she couldn't stop, as she watched the cow pitching stiff-legged through the weeds, bawling, and breaking the string from Harry's hands.

Henry and Teddy could barely stand up for the giggling.

"Don't you hurt that kite, cow!" Henry laughed, just as the animal at last dislodged her paper hat under a mesquite limb and trampled it into the ground.

Still grinning, Nita turned back to the Spam.

There was something different about the way her boys played with a man—different from the way they played with her or with each other. She had noticed it sometimes when they played with Mr. Bailey, inasmuch as the poor crippled man could play at all, but the air was electric with it this afternoon—an excitement, as if there were more at stake than met the eye of a mother looking on casually from the kitchen window, as if the rules of the game had been pulled a notch tighter. . . .

With a start, Nita realized she could suddenly see them both—Harry and her baby, Henry— as young men, as builders of kites for other boys, perhaps (she shuddered) as sailors soon to sail away in warships over the glazed black sea. That was what gave this play with men its voltage—the knowledge that it was only half-play, that the other half, the part that drove them to run faster and longer and to jump higher and farther, wasn't play at all—not play, but kind of ritual learning, a preparation for all those things of manhood, barely under-stood, that were yet to come for them.

Her boys would one day, not really so very long from now, be men.

When she went to the door a few minutes later to call them to the table, Teddy and the boys were already crossing the road to the house, laughing and talking.

When Teddy looked up, she waved, and he waved back at the smiling woman in the pink doorway.

"Supper's ready," she called. Then, as soon as the switchboard buzzed, she was gone.

Teddy's steps slowed as his mind moved through the empty doorway, fingering the edges of some memory just out of reach. Supper's ready. Long-tailed kites and rubberband boats. Kids and cows in a vacant lot. A woman in the doorway. Things the Navy had made him forget. He stopped at the edge of the yard and watched the two boys bound up the steps to the porch.

"Oh boy!" cried Harry. "Spam for supper!" He turned around. "Hey, Teddy!" he called. "Smell the Spam!"

Kids. He and Charlotte had never gotten around to talking about kids, but he'd always assumed they'd have some—maybe four or five. Charlotte . . . he had almost forgotten for a little while. So pretty and so sweet to come home to. Supper cooking on the stove, a half-embroidered pillowcase in its hoop on the arm of the couch, stockings drying on a bathroom rack. Charlotte . . .

Henry was giggling and bouncing in his chair. "Never saw a cow jump like that!" he laughed, swooping his fork exuberantly through his mashed potatoes.

"Hey diddle diddle, the cat and the fiddle," recited Teddy with a grin, "the cow jumped over the moon!"

"Yeah!" giggled Henry.

Even Nita had to laugh again, that strange feeling bubbling up inside her.

"What're we gonna do tomorrow, Teddy?" Harry grinned.

"Well," Teddy said slowly, "I'm afraid I'm gonna have to go back tonight, Harry. . . ." He wished he'd thought ahead, realized this moment was bound to come, prepared for it better.

Harry's grin disappeared.

"No, Teddy!" Henry dropped a forkful of potatoes on the tablecloth. "Don't go!"

Teddy looked from Harry to Henry. "I'm sorry," he said gently.

"Aw, *Teddy!*" said Harry, pushing back his plate. "You don't *have* to go!" He turned his stricken eyes on his mother's face. "Does he, Mama?"

Nita hesitated just a moment before her son's gaze. She looked up at Teddy. "It's fine with me," she smiled, "if you want to stay."

There it was again, that something familiar, just out of consciousness, just out of reach, something Charlotte . . . Teddy smiled back at her.

"Will you?" cried Harry, jumping up from his chair, his whole face a huge grin.

"Yeah!" cried Henry eagerly. "Will you?"

"Well," said Teddy, twirling his water glass and looking at Nita.

"Come on, Teddy!" Harry pleaded, pulling Teddy's sleeve. "Mama!" he begged.

Nita smiled at him and then at Teddy. "We . . ." she hesitated. "All three of us . . . really would like for you to stay."

"Yeah!" said Henry.

"Well . . ." said Teddy again. If some memories refused to come closer, others crowded in: the base with its obsession of rows and lines; its unbearable paper-and-leather tasting food; the close smell of hundreds of men confined, of the officers angry or depressed; of the kids like him, dazed, scared; the huge hollow ships that, struck by the darkness of the waves, sounded like war gongs and alarm bells, so that your whole body shook from without and within alike from the force and its echo; the ever-present crushing power of the deep and the death by water or fire that could (would) come from anywhere, everywhere, any time, forevermore. . . .

"I'm still on my leave . . ." he said hesitantly.

"Hot dog!" yelled Harry, grabbing Teddy's arm. "You mean it? You'll stay?"

Teddy met Nita's smile, shrugged his shoulders a little self-consciously, and nodded.

"Hot diggity dog!" Henry kicked the table from underneath with a metallic clang.

It was almost like a family, Teddy thought, the four of them. Not exactly the family he'd anticipated, when he'd planned to see Charlotte, maybe ask her to marry him, ask Mr. Shinn's permission . . .

But that was all over, he reminded himself with a shake of his head.

"Okay," Nita laughed. "That's settled. Now you boys go get ready for bed."

Pushing his chair back from the table, Henry glanced at Nita to see if she had noticed the little pile of mashed potatoes on the tablecloth by his plate.

"Teddy," said Harry with a smile, "are you gonna be our daddy?"

"Harry!" Nita gasped.

Teddy glanced up, embarrassed.

Henry very carefully set his milk glass squarely over the potatoes, smashing them into a flat white circle.

"I was just asking, Mama," said Harry. Why

was she so upset? Why had Teddy's face turned red? Harry looked at his mother, confused.

"Well," said Nita, pulling him to her for a goodnight hug, "that's *not* the kind of question you ask somebody. Now y'all run on to bed."

"Okay, Mama," Harry murmured as he returned her hug. Why wasn't it a question you could ask?

As Henry dived for Nita's arms and his own goodnight kiss, Harry turned to Teddy, still worried. Why wasn't it?

But with a grin, Teddy held out his arms. "Goodnight, Harry," he said, embracing the boy warmly, feeling the thin arms around his neck, the warm breath on his cheek, as Henry leaned toward him from the other side, burying his face in Teddy's shirt front.

"Goodnight, boys," he said, hugging them both and smiling at Nita over the tops of their heads. He was glad he was staying.

"Oh boy!" yelled Henry, scampering for the bedroom. "Teddy's gonna stay!"

Harry followed slowly, rubbing his cheek. He had forgotten how that felt, whiskers, when you hugged someone. . . .

A few minutes later, after the boys had gone out to the privy and then to bed, Teddy pulled shut the door to the back room and sat down on the edge of Nita's cot.

"Today's sure been fun for me," he said.

"For the boys too," she smiled, finishing a call at the switchboard. "They don't have much of anybody to play with. Mr. Bailey's about all."

"Poor guy," Teddy shook his head. "His face . . ."

"His looks don't bother the boys."

Teddy glanced up at her shyly. "I don't mean to pry," he began, "but . . . where's their daddy?"

Nita turned slowly back toward the switchboard.

"We got divorced," she said. "Four years ago . . ." She sighed painfully to herself. "Lord, that long . . ."

"I'm sorry," he murmured. "It's none of my business."

"No, that's all right." She smiled softly, but her back was still to him. "He drank too much, played too hard . . . that sort of thing. I took the boys and left. Came here eventually and got this job. I figured anything'd be better than all that."

"That's a shame," said Teddy sympathetically.

"Yes and no." Nita shrugged her shoulders. "Still, I kinda wish he'd write or something . . . you know. Mostly for Harry's sake. Henry was just a baby when we got divorced. He doesn't remember anything. But Harry was old enough to know he had a daddy. . . . He remembers the fun parts." Nita laughed. Poor Harry. "He keeps a lot of things inside him." Sometimes she wondered if she had been selfish to get the divorce, too wrapped up in her own disappointments and angers to have realized how much it would hurt her older boy.

"In his own way," she said sadly, "he keeps watching for his daddy to come home—every bit as hard as Henry watches for Japs." She looked down at her hands in her lap.

Teddy caught the note of regret in her voice, the pain she had hardly admitted even to herself. Everybody has problems. A few minutes ago he'd felt lucky to have stumbled into such a happy little family, a friendly, cheerful woman, two energetic kids, at a time when he needed encouragement, reassurance. And now, now he was wishing there was something he could do to cheer them up, to reassure this same friendly, pretty woman that everything was really Okay.

"Listen," he said suddenly. "What would you think if I took the boys over to Corpus tomorrow for a picture show?" He wondered why he hadn't thought of this before.

Nita looked up surprised.

"It's just seventeen miles," he went on eagerly. "We could go on the bus."

"Oh, they'd love it!" Nita said, breaking into a grin. "Neither one of them has ever been to a picture show!"

"Any chance of you going with us?" he smiled warmly.

A blaring buzz from the switchboard and the blinking light gave him his answer. Nita grimaced as she plugged in the cord.

"I wish there was. . . ." she said sadly.

He nodded.

"Number please . . ." she said.

At the door to the front room, Teddy waved a silent goodnight to her as she worked the call. It was nice to see her smile in response.

As he pulled the door to, the front room fell into darkness. Tomorrow would be fun.

Outside, the man's figure watching from the vacant lot could no longer see Teddy, only Nita's shape seated at the switchboard under the unshaded light.

10

"You're Harry, the Sa-a-i--ilor Ma-a-an!" Teddy sang, pulling his cap down over his eye and winking.

Harry looked at their reflections in the store's long wavy mirror between the racks and racks of pants and shirts: they wore three identical white sailor suits and three white sailor caps on their blond heads. Turning to Henry with a grin, he saluted.

Giggling, Henry saluted back. "Aye-aye, sir!"

Lichtenstein's was the biggest store Harry had ever been in, right in the middle of the biggest town he'd ever seen.

"Come on! Get up!" Teddy had yelled that morning. "We've got to get moving if we're going to Corpus!"

"Where?" Harry had stammered, sitting bolt upright in bed.

"To Corpus!" Teddy repeated.

"Corpus!" Henry had cried, jumping up and down on his bed.

"Yeah, Corpus!" Teddy grabbed Henry and swooped him to the floor. "We're gonna go see a picture show and stuff our faces full of popcorn!"

A picture show!

And then . . . the bus bigger than the house! The thousands of people swarming the intersections of the streets filled from curb to curb with cars and trucks! The acres of sandy beach into which they tackled Teddy, giggling and whooping! The foot-long hotdogs that oozed sunny-yellow mustard and cheese and hot red chili all over their faces! The mysteriously adult pinball machines that only men played, decorated with pink and yellow girls in bathing suits under palm trees or with ferocious airplane-tank battles which raged through the buzzers, bells, and blinking lights, as the metal ball clunked through the maze!

And now—the sailor suits! Harry knew the square collar and bell-bottom pants had instantly initiated him into the brotherhood of the military. Now he could salute the uniformed men they passed in the streets and the men would have to salute back, because of the white sailor suit with stars on the sleeves and the knotted tie.

Stepping from the strange revolving door of the store back into the crowded sidewalk, he tried it. Sure enough, a man in brown khakis saluted back with a grin!

"Can we see your ship, Teddy?" he asked, as

the three of them saluted two approaching white-clad officers.

"Sure," Teddy smiled. "Let's go."

As they climbed the tall bridge across the bay, Harry's mouth fell open at the sight of the hundreds of naval ships, small as toys, clotting the water below them. He felt dizzy looking down.

"Wow!" said Henry, swinging on the rails. "Which one's yours, Teddy?"

"I don't know," he answered, staring into the drowsing flotilla below. "They don't tell us too much . . ." His voice trailed off.

All three of them looked out across the sun-danced water as it widened beyond the bay into a deeper blue and filled the whole horizon of the world. It spilled over, they knew, beyond, to lap just like this into the bays and under the bridges of Europe, of Africa, and somewhere out there, farther still, of the islands of Japan.

"Is that where you're going, Teddy?" Harry asked in a hushed whisper, squinting against his dizziness toward the farthest white-capped reaches of the water.

"I won't know that either," Teddy said softly, taking Harry's hand. "They don't tell us much at all."

"Are there Japs out there?" asked Henry, excited.

"Well," Teddy smiled, "probably not right down there. But somewhere out there, yes, there are Japs. . . ."

"Are you gonna kill some Japs?" Henry asked.

Teddy patted him on the head. "I don't know, Henry, I just don't know."

As swells of dizziness reeled about Harry's knees, he held tightly to Teddy's hand. He didn't want to think anymore about Japs or little ships or bottomless oceans of water or being so high up in the air like this, so far from everything he knew about, looking down with nothing under him.

He felt for a moment like a balloon, filled with a light-headed gas and about to float away. Mama!

Teddy squeezed his hand and led him back down the walk.

"You all ready to see that picture show now?" he grinned.

"Yea!" bellowed Henry, and Harry nodded as they stepped back on the plain hard ground he was used to.

In a few minutes they were waiting, dazzled, before the blue mirror-glazed façade of the picture show as Teddy bought their tickets.

"Thirty-five cents for you," said the blue-haired lady behind the barred window. "And seven cents each for the kids."

When the heavy velvet curtain lumbered up on squeaky chains and the first flickers of light appeared on the screen, Harry giggled with pleasure and heard Henry, on the other side of Teddy, guffaw. A real picture show!

"The March of Time," he read aloud from the letters that filled the screen.

"What's that?" he asked Teddy.

"Shhh!" said Teddy. "It's the news."

Henry sat on the edge of his seat, wide-eyed.

A whole yardful of men were stomping, stiff-legged across the screen. "Heil Hitler!" they boomed, so loud it made him jump.

"They sure walk funny!" he snickered.

Harry laughed, stuffing a handful of popcorn in his mouth, eyes glued to the high-stepping figures before him.

"Shhh!" Teddy whispered to Henry. "That's called goose-stepping."

"What?" Henry giggled.

"Goose-stepping!" Teddy repeated his whisper.

"Goose-stepping!" Henry bellowed, laughing incredulously as the Nazi soldiers crossed the screen again from the other direction.

"Shhh!" Teddy threatened, as Harry dug into his popcorn box and watched the moving beam of light jump across the surface of the screen.

Then as suddenly as they appeared, the soldiers were gone, replaced by pictures of a baseball game. Joe DiMaggio, the announcer said, hit two more home runs. And there he was, rounding third base in his striped suit with the number 5 on the back, heading for home with a big grin, while somewhere a band they couldn't see was playing "Take Me Out to the Ba-a-all Ga-a-ame . . ."

After the screen went dark for a minute and Harry was afraid the picture show was over, some new words appeared.

"John Wayne . . ." he read.

"Who's that?" Henry asked.

"Shhh!" Teddy hissed. "He's the movie star."

"In *The Flying Tigers*," Harry read.

"Oh boy!" cried Henry. "Tigers!"

"Shhh!" said Teddy.

"Shhh!" hissed a man sitting in the row behind them.

But there were no tigers in the picture show, they soon found out. Only airplanes with hideous painted-on teeth and eyes and the men who flew inside them.

"And Japs!" Henry yelled, when the first slant-eyed, grinning, buck-toothed villain appeared.

"Shhh!" said the man in the row behind.

"Whisper!" Teddy whispered.

Men, airplanes, Japs, and . . . something else, something Henry hadn't known much about before—something called Death.

The P-40s swooped like angry wasps, their jaggedly painted teeth bared in vicious hunger, their cold round eyes pinning the Zeros against the smoke-stained, flattened sky as the guns spat out their fury.

On the edge of his heat, Henry watched, excited, grinning, kicking the seat in front of him.

And then, with horrible suddenness, his mouth fell open as a bullet found the soft fleshy heart of one of the Zeros, and he watched the Japanese pilot's no-longer-grinning face contort in the violence of surprised pain. Tightly gripping the back of the seat in front, Henry stood up, crushing the popcorn box at his feet.

Dark blood spurted from the grimacing mouth and ears, as the Jap's head rolled helplessly to one side and his limp hands fell from the controls of the plane like a bird Henry had once seen Emile Lucas shoot from a tree with a B-B gun. He stared in disbelief. Emile Lucas, whom his Mama had told him was dead now.

With a whine, the plane spun out of control, mindless, arcing heavily toward the water below in a trail of smoke and a spray of blood.

Banking his nearby P-40, John Wayne smiled his trumph as the screaming Zero exploded in a boiling flame and was no more, not wings, nor fuselage, nor tail, nor pilot's seat, nor man with the bloody face and the squinted-shut, slanted eyes. Gone. Shot. Burned up. Dead. Gone. John Wayne's plane grinned through its painted teeth.

Stunned, Henry had forgotten Teddy, forgotten Harry, forgotten he was in a picture show in Corpus, forgotten everything but the images that flashed before his round blue eyes.

Teddy touched him on the back. "Henry?"

With a start, Henry turned.

"Okay, Henry?" Teddy asked.

But Henry could only blink and swallow. It didn't really seem okay. He sat down again, as two nastily smiling Japanese pilots swung after John Wayne, firing what Henry now understood were bullets that could make you dead. With a wail, he ducked down below the seat, terrified, unable to look.

"Did they get him?"

"Not yet," Teddy said tensely, his own eyes riveted to the screen.

"Shhh!" said the man behind.

When, after a minute, Henry dared to look again, he was met with another blast of deadly fire from the Japanese guns. Covering his eyes in his newly born fear, he ducked his head again.

"Did they get him? Did they get him?" he demanded from behind the seat.

"Not yet," Teddy whispered. "Not yet."

When he next looked up, John Wayne's P-40 was diving in a long swoop toward the ground, its snarling mouth aimed at the waves below.

"They're gonna get him," he said sadly, pillowing his head on his arms and sinking below the back of the seat once more. He could already see the blood pouring thickly from John Wayne's strong, handsome mouth, his eyes glazing over, his goggled head falling loosely forward on his chest. . . .

Henry didn't open his tear-stung eyes again until the lights came on.

Stumbling out with the crowd, holding Teddy's hand, he looked up. "They got him, didn't they?" he sniffled.

"No," Teddy smiled, squeezing his hand. "He got them!"

"Really?" He looked suspiciously first at Harry and then at Teddy.

"Really!" Teddy said.

He got them! But before Henry could smile, the thought of the two Japanese pilots brought him close to tears again. He got them! Henry could see their slack, bloody mouths, their useless fingers, their skin growing cold and hard as the dead bird had.

He felt his own arm. Warm. Not skinny black lines on a piece of folded-up paper he could stuff in his pocket. But real. Like him.

Like John Wayne. Like Teddy. They could've gotten him, but he got them. They could've gotten him . . . Henry stumbled against Teddy's leg.

"Hey, captain," said Teddy, as he bent over in the carpeted foyer of the theater and picked Henry up. He balanced him on his hip with an arm around his waist, holding Harry's hand on the other side. "How about a Coke before we catch the bus home?"

Henry wiped his eyes and threw both arms around Teddy's neck. "Can I have an Orange Crush?" he sniffed.

"Sure," Teddy grinned, "Here comes an officer," he whispered as they stepped out onto the sidewalk. "Better salute!"

And as the Navy lieutenant came abreast of the uniformed threesome, they all saluted smartly.

Harry looked around, surprised. It was dark out. Beyond the glare of the hundreds of little light bulbs under the over-hanging blue-mirrored marquee, the bright sunny afternoon had turned to full night while they were inside.

He squeezed Teddy's hand. What an *unbelievable* day!

11

Nita wasn't used to being alone in the house at night without the boys. No voices from the back room, no jars full of lightning bugs captured as the sun went down, no "Hi-yo, Silver!" wafting tinnily from the radio as Henry rode his maroon plush steed of the couch arm into the gathering darkness.

She stepped out the back door into the dark yard and smiled as she thought of Teddy, wondering if he bit off more than he could chew, having to ride herd on both of them all day long.

She pulled open the privy door and latched it behind her. "Is Teddy going to be our daddy?" Poor Harry had looked so surprised when she jumped on him for that one.

Recrossing the back yard toward the house, she glanced up as a pair of headlights down by the highway swung their beams through the brush of the vacant lot where the cow grazed. What? Nita froze. What was that? In the vacant lot. Something was there. Someone! There, in that vague light, not only the shape of the cow in the back part of the lot, but also, closer to this side, closer to her, she was sure it had been the figure of a man, head and shoulders a dark shadow against the passing glare.

The light was gone.

Sudden fear pricking her feet, Nita dashed for the back door and locked it behind her. She quickly turned out the light in the back room and peered out the window toward the road, but, in the full darkness, could see nothing in the vacant lot, not even the cow or the brush she knew was there.

Of course, it was nothing, her imagination, just from being alone for a change, some branches and leaves against the summer night. But her heart was beating too fast and her breath coming too quickly to convince herself that the shape had been anything so insubstantial. In the middle room she hesitantly picked up the headset and, after glancing once at the black square of the window, plugged in the cord.

"Sheriff Watson? This is Nita Longley and I'm sorry to bother you, but . . . well, I think someone's trying to window peek over here. ... ."

This was silly. Usually with Harry and Henry running around like little heathens, laughing and playing, she didn't have time to think about things like this. She wasn't used to it.

"Yes, sir," she went on. "I think I saw somebody standing across the street, just standing there."

"I sure would appreciate it," she said, relieved when he offered to come check it out. "Thank you."

A few minutes later she saw his car drive slowly past the house, flashing a spotlight over the vacant lot. There was the cow again, staring stupidly at the sudden intrusion. But no figure of a man.

The sheriff's car pulled to a stop in front and Nita went to the door.

"I didn't see nobody, Mrs. Longley," the sheriff said, shifting the shotgun to his left hand and removing his hat as he stepped inside.

"Well, I sure think there was somebody out there."

"Coulda been," Sheriff Watson nodded. "But they gone now if they were. Nothing out there now but one old cow." He smiled in a fatherly way.

"I appreciate your looking," said Nita. "It just kinda scared me."

"Well, don't never hesitate to call up. You keep a gun around here?"

"No, sir," Nita shook her head, "I don't." Guns had never been something she wanted to have around the house, what with the boys being boys and all.

"Wouldn't hurt none to have one," the sheriff grunted, holding out the shotgun to her. "You can't never tell. Had to take this one offa Meskin. It ain't worth much but it works. Took a fella's head off at the neck with it. . . ."

"Oh! . . ." Nita gasped, drawing her hand back.

"Aw, I don't mean me," Sheriff Watson said. "I mean the Meskin. He did it." He pushed it toward her again.

"It's loaded," he warned, as she took it awkwardly in both hands.

"Well . . ." murmured Nita, looking at the gun as if it were a piece of matter from another planet.

"Anybody come messing around here, you just point and pull. That's what I do," he said, pulling open the front door. "You won't have no more trouble." He jammed his hat back on his head as he stepped out on the porch.

"Now you just telephone me up if you get scared over here," he said.

"I will," Nita nodded, still holding the alien shotgun. "Thank you, Sheriff Watson."

She locked the door behind him and stared at the cold metal. A place to keep it, a place where nobody could get hurt by it. She carried it stiffly into the middle room. There! Behind the switchboard—the boys already knew not to play in here.

With the gun safely out of sight, she stepped once again to the darkened square of the back room window and stared into the overgrown lot, watching for a shape, a movement, any hint that would confirm the certainty she felt: that there *had* been something out there besides the one old cow.

12

Henry stood up on the bus seat to be sure Teddy and Harry were in the seats right behind. They were. Sinking back to his knees, he examined the older man in the seat next to him by the window.

"Hi!" said Henry, leaning over toward him with a grin.

The man glanced sourly in Henry's direction and returned his gaze to the window.

"I said, 'Hi!'" Henry repeated, leaning over until he was almost in the man's lap.

Glaring toward the boy, the man shifted his weight. "Hi," he finally said, in a voice as cold as his eyes.

Henry straightened up, grinning, but the man turned back to the window.

"My name's Henry," he offered. When the man made no response, he gave his full name. "Henry Lee Longley. That's my name."

For the first time, the man's glare met Henry's with a hint of interest.

"What's your name?" Henry asked seriously.

"I told you my name."

"Voss," said the man.

"*Voss*?" Henry whooped. "Your name's *Voss*?"

"It's my *last* name," the man said, irritated.

"Oh," said Henry nodding. "What's your other name?"

"My *first* name?" the man asked.

Henry nodded.

Looking around to see if he would be overheard, the man leaned over. "Dudley," he whispered.

"What?" cried Henry.

"Dudley!" hissed the man.

"That's as funny as your other name!" Henry whooped again. "Wow! Dudley Voss!"

Giving Henry another sour look, the man turned back to the window. He reached into his pocket and pulled out a cigar.

"Can I have the band?" Henry asked quickly.

Without glancing at the boy, the man handed him the band. It was dark red and gold with scrolly writing.

"See, now I got a ring!" Henry said, holding up his hand with the band on his middle finger.

The man stuck the cigar in his mouth without answering.

"We been to Corpus Christi, Dudley," Henry went on, examining his ring. "We saw a picture show . . ." He paused. "All the Japs got kilt."

"Yeah?" said the man without interest, chewing on his cigar.

"Yeah . . ." said Henry, his new confusing knowledge of mortality clouding his voice. "Do you know about that?" he asked. "About people getting kilt?"

"Hey," the bus driver called. "There's no smoking cigars on the bus!"

The man looked up angrily in the driver's direction, but said nothing.

"The name of the picture show was *Flying Tigers*," Henry went on. "But it wasn't about flying tigers. It was about killing Japs. . . ." He looked up at the man. "Another part was about goose-stepping. Do you know what that is? Goose-stepping?"

"I said," the bus driver yelled again, glaring into the rearview mirror, "there's no smoking cigars allowed on the bus."

Once again, the man eyed the bus driver coldly, but did not remove his cigar.

"Hey, Dudley," Henry offered helpfully, "the driver said you can't smoke on the bus."

There was no response.

"Dudley? . . ." said Henry.

"I heard him," said the man, exasperated, taking out his cigar and extending the chewed end toward Henry. "I'm not smoking. I'm chewing! See?"

"Oh," said Henry, surprised, examining the end of the cigar, "why aren't you smoking it?"

"Because," the man said, even more irritated, "there's no smoking allowed on the bus!"

"Oh yeah," Henry grinned. "That's right."

The man stuck the chewed cigar back into his mouth.

"Mister!" yelled the bus driver angrily into the

rearview mirror. "I said there's no cigar smoking allowed!"

As the man jerked his cigar out angrily, Henry grabbed it from his hand. Sliding out of his seat, he walked slowly up the swaying aisle, holding onto the seat arms, until he stood beside the driver.

"He's not smoking," Henry explained, holding out the end of the cigar for inspection. "He's chewing, look!"

The bus driver looked at the cold cigar.

"Anything wrong with chewing cigars on this bus?" Henry asked, his lower lip stuck out and one hand on his hip.

"Well, no," the bus driver shook his head. "I guess not. . . ."

Henry marched back to his seat and held out the cigar to the man by the window.

"You can go on and chew it if you want to, Dudley," he smiled.

"I sure do thank you," grinned Dudley, taking the cigar. Spunky kid.

"That's okay," said Henry as he climbed back into his seat. He held his red and gold paper ring up to the little light over the seat.

"You got any boys, Dudley?" he asked.

The cigar stopped halfway to the man's mouth.

"No," he said softly.

"Really?" Henry settled back.

"No," the man shook his head. "No, I don't have any boys."

"I bet you wish you had some boys," Henry said, smiling up at the man, who studied him for a moment and then turned back toward

89

the window. "Some boys to give your rings to,"
Henry added. "Don't you, Dudley? Don't you
wish you had some boys?"

"I . . . I had a boy," the man said at last, his
face still turned toward the window.

"Really?" said Henry.

"Yes, I did," the man nodded. "I had a boy."

"And you don't have him any more, Dudley?"
Henry asked.

"No," the man said softly, "I don't have him
any more."

"Why not, Dudley?" Henry asked, leaning
over to try to see his face again.

"I . . . just don't. . . ." the man replied, Henry
could see he was biting his lip.

"Well, *where* is he?" Henry insisted.

"He was . . . lost in the war. . . ." Dudley
almost whispered.

Henry sat back in his seat.

"You mean he's . . . *dead*?" He studied the
back of the man's head, trying to understand.
"He got kilt?"

"Yes," the man nodded.

Without warning, the vision spurted into
Henry's mind: the blood, as sudden as a thun-
derclap, gushing from the mouth, the ears of
a small boy, a boy not at all unlike himself.
The boy's hand fell limply to his side, like the
cold, feathery wing of a dead bird. A boy like
Henry . . .

Henry wished the man would turn around
and make the picture disappear, tell him it was
okay. But the man kept his face to the window
and then Henry saw a tear fall from the man's
cheek to the sleeve of his shirt. With a sniff,

the man rubbed at the spot with a finger.

Henry blinked away the boy's pale face, the bird's stiff foot.

"That's sad, Dudley," he said. He reached out and touched the man's arm. "I guess a lot of people are getting kilt." There was Emile Lucas . . . and the Japs in the picture show . . . and now Dudley's boy. . . .

The man sniffed again.

"But I bet you were glad to have a boy when you had a boy," said Henry.

There was no response for a minute. Then, "Yes," the man said softly, "I was . . ."

"Even if you had a boy for only a little while, I bet you were glad," said Henry.

When the man turned toward him, his eyes were wet.

"Yes," the man nodded. "Even for a little while I guess I was glad." He smiled and nodded more vigorously. "I was. Yes, I was."

Henry grinned up at him. "I'll be your boy for a little while, Dudley," he said, snuggling against the man's arm. "Until I get home. Then I've got to be my mama's boy."

When the bus stopped in Gregory and Teddy reached into the seat to pick up Henry, sound asleep, the man turned from the window where he'd been staring into the darkened street.

"He's asleep," he whispered to Teddy.

"He had a big day," Teddy smiled, hoisting Henry's limp body to his shoulder. The red and gold paper ring slid unnoticed to the floor.

"He's a fine little fella," the man said.

"Sure is," Teddy nodded.

Harry stood behind Teddy, leaning sleepily against his leg.

"When he wakes up," the man said, "you tell him the man with the cigar said thanks."

Teddy looked at him curiously.

"Just tell him that. Tell him thanks." The man smiled.

Teddy nodded, shifted Henry's weight higher on his shoulder, and led Harry off the bus.

13

Nita and Teddy undressed the two sleeping boys.

"These are the cutest outfits I ever saw," Nita grinned, folding up the white pants and blouses. "You shouldn't have done that."

"Listen," Teddy laughed, as Henry saluted in his sleep. "I was glad to do it." He liked seeing her happy.

"Want some coffee?" Nita asked. She switched out the light. "I bet you had a hard day too."

"I sure do. Those boys'll wear a fella out." He pulled the door to. "But it was fun," he said.

Climbing the steps to the porch a few minutes ago, with Henry asleep on his shoulder and Harry's tired hand in his, he had recognized that feeling again. When Nita had released the chain lock and swung the door open wide, he had realized what it was her smile told him —coming home. He was coming home.

Once he stepped through that door, all the troubles of his world fell away. Here he was safe, as he slipped into the circle. Charlotte? He could hardly remember who that was. The war? Oh, maybe it was out there someplace still. But it couldn't touch him here. . . .

He watched her rounded back and arms as she reached the cups down off their hooks and the sugar from the top shelf.

"It was more fun than I've had in a real long time," he added.

"They'll be talking about it for weeks," she smiled, pouring the coffee.

When the switchboard buzzed, she smiled at Teddy and shrugged her shoulders as she reached for the headset.

"Number please," she said, sitting down. "Just a moment. I'll connect you." She inserted the cord.

"I don't see how you stand it," said Teddy sympathetically, handing her the coffee cup, "working those calls night and day."

"I don't have much choice," she sighed.

Teddy sat down on the cot. "You could find a different job," he said.

"I could," said Nita, turning to face him. "But I'm frozen in this one."

"That can't be right," said Teddy, surprised. "You mean to tell me you can't quit?"

"Not until the war's over or till I get off the Agency's—the State Employment Agency's—frozen list. Otherwise, it's against the law." She sipped at her coffee.

"I didn't have any idea they could do that,"

he mused, looking at her with a new consciousness of her predicament.

"They can in wartime," she said. "They can do *anything* in wartime."

"Brother!" He shook his head. How naïve he'd been, thinking the war couldn't reach into here, couldn't march right through the door or crawl in the windows. It was everywhere.

The switchboard light came on and Nita reached for the cord to disconnect it.

Teddy rubbed his eyes. Poor Nita. Such a fine lady. And poor kids. If only he wasn't shipping out so soon. . . .

"You must be tired," she said gently.

"A little," he admitted. "Henry's heavier'n he looks."

"Want some more coffee?"

"I can get it," he said, standing up. "Want some?"

"About half a cup," she nodded, holding out her cup.

As Teddy reached for it, he was at that instant very aware of her fingers curling under the bottom of the china cup, passing through the handle. His hand closed tentatively, awkwardly around hers, so that together they were holding the cup. He could tell that his hand was shaking. Nita . . .

She looked up at him, surprised, and then looked back at their hands.

When he squeezed her fingers just a little bit, she looked at him again, wide-eyed, afraid. Lips parted, she drew a slow, shaky breath.

Still looking into her eyes, he leaned over and

95

kissed her, feeling her sharp intake of breath. Such a fine lady.

Nita stood up slowly and Teddy pulled her to him, still holding her hand and the coffee cup between them.

"Teddy . . ." she whispered, eyes closed, lips trembling.

He kissed her again and then took a step backwards, leading her toward him. She followed, and he pulled her down beside him on the cot.

She gazed into his eyes, unblinking. Her look was almost desperate, before she closed her eyes and kissed him more passionately than he had ever been kissed.

Teddy tightened his embrace. Oh, Nita . . .

The man watching from the vacant lot across the road could no longer see the two figures on the cot, but he could hear the raucous buzz of the switchboard when it called. And he understood the meaning when the buzzing continued, impatient, but unheeded in the otherwise silent night. From the vacant lot, the man—Mr. Bailey—listened to the buzzing for another minute and then, hands in his pockets and head down, stumbled sadly away. The cow lifted her head to stare after him, as the brush caught at his clothes and the weeds grabbed his lurching feet.

On the cot by the buzzing switchboard, Teddy felt Nita stiffen. He kissed her again, but she sat up.

"I better get it," she said, smiling at him apologetically.

"Number please?" she said into the headset, as she sat down in the chair.

Teddy sat up too. It was quiet now that the rude buzzing had stopped.

"Just a moment," said Nita, pulling out the directory, "I'll see if we have a listing under that name."

Teddy listened to her turn the pages. He listened to the insects outside.

"That number is three-four," she said. "I'll connect you."

She plugged in the cord, but she didn't turn around. In a minute she'd have to disconnect the monster.

He heard her sigh, and when he looked up he could see that her shoulders were shaking. Nita was crying. He looked sadly at the floor. Damn this shark-toothed war!

"I'm sorry," she said softly a minute later. She unplugged the cord and turned around.

He looked up into her troubled eyes. Their moment was gone, too fragile . . . too ephemeral . . . gone.

He looked away, alone.

"Me too, Nita," he whispered to the night.

14

"Goodbye, Mr. Buford." Harry, in his new white sailor suit, turned and saluted the grocer. Then he straightened out the handle of the loaded wagon and pulled it through the door onto the sidewalk.

"Thanks, Mr. Buford," said Henry around the mouthful of jellybeans, as he too saluted. Outside, he steadied the bags, as they both peered down the block toward the corner where they were supposed to meet Teddy when he got back from the post office.

There was no matching white suit in sight yet.

But there *was* the Triplett brothers' cattle truck parked at the curb.

Pulling the wheels carefully across the crack in the sidewalk, Harry was determined not to look in the poolhall door. He told himself that his daddy wouldn't be in there anyway. He never had been, in all the times Harry had looked for him. But he knew that mostly he was afraid of seeing the two pool players who he was pretty sure *would* be there.

Sure enough. When he looked up from the broken pavement, there, in the middle of the sidewalk in front of the sinful door, were Calvin's scuffed and broken boots, blocking the way.

"Well now, goddam," Calvin leered drunkenly, beer bottle and pool cue in hand. "Would you just lookee here! These damn boys went and joined the goddam Navy!"

Arnold filled the doorway, laughing.

"Damn if they didn't! Look at them little miniature sailor suits!"

Harry, taking a step back, looked for Teddy down at the corner. "Y'all better get outta the way!" he said apprehensively.

"Aw now," chided Calvin, "we're just trying to be friendly."

"Y'all better come on in and have a beer before y'all ship out," Arnold laughed.

"Harry told y'all before," said Henry impatiently, hands on his hips, "we're too young to be drinking beer."

"Well, then," said Arnold, "how about a cold bottle of Orange Crush?"

Harry could feel Henry's interest.

"Come on, Henry," he said anxiously, "We gotta go."

"Aw hell, sailor boy," said Calvin, sticking the pool cue under the wheels of the wagon, "park that wagon and come on in here and we'll treat y'all to a big ol' bottle of Orange Crush."

"Ain't often we treat," said Arnold.

"Goddam," laughed Calvin, "if that ain't the truth."

Harry felt the worry begin to climb the inside of his stomach on its little rat feet. He wished he were home lying in bed, watching the horse rearing on the ceiling, or feeling the smooth hard coolness of the colored eggs safe in their white china basket.

"I'd sure take an Orange Crush," Henry said.

"There you go!" Calvin winked at Arnold.

"We better not, Henry." Desperation tensed Harry's voice.

"Aw now, y'all come on in here and we'll set 'em right up," said Calvin, patting Henry on the back.

"Hell, yeah," said Arnold, "y'all come on." He stepped aside to let them enter.

"Come on, Harry!" Henry smiled as he passed through the doorway, followed by Calvin and Arnold.

Harry knew he couldn't let Henry go alone. Not here. Not with *them*. He looked once more down the street for Teddy and then reluctantly parked the wagon by the door. Feeling the scratching fear in his stomach, he entered the dingy poolhall.

"Let's, by God, have a couple of them Orange Crushes for these sailor boys," Arnold called, slapping the bar. "They're about to ship out!"

Frowning, Crecencio opened two bottles of Orange Crush and set them on the bar. He folded his arms across his chest and leaned back against the cold box, eyeing Arnold and Calvin. Why didn't they leave these kids alone, he wondered.

Arnold grabbed Henry under the arms and set him on the bar beside his bottle, and Calvin lifted Harry onto the bar next to him.

"Now then, how them drinks?" Calvin grinned.

"Just fine," said Henry, rubbing his mouth on his white sleeve. He looked in alarm at the orange smear.

Harry took a nervous sip from his bottle.

"Well, don't drink 'em too fast," Arnold hooted. "They'll make you drunk as a coot. Your mama might not like it if you two was to come home shit-faced drunk!"

Calvin laughed, as Harry sipped at his drink again, his eyes darting warily from one of the Triplett brothers to the other.

"We been thinking about coming over and paying your mama a little visit," said Calvin, eyeing Henry. "Whatta y'all think she'd say to that?"

Crecencio cleared his throat loudly.

"She don't even know y'all," said Henry, lowering his bottle.

"Well, we been thinking she might take a shine to us," Arnold grinned, winking at Calvin.

"No, she wouldn't!" Harry answered emphatically.

"Shoot!" Calvin laughed, poking Harry with an elbow. "Couple good-looking fellas like us?"

"Y'all ain't good-looking," Henry scoffed. "Y'all don't even brush your teeth!" He turned his bottle up again.

"Ain't our teeth we'd be showing your mama," Calvin leered.

"By God!" Arnold slapped the bar, giggling. "That's right, ain't it!"

Crecencio stood up. "Don't fool with them boys that ways," he said.

No one answered him.

Harry didn't like any of this. He glanced at the bartender and tried to slide off the bar, only to find Arnold standing in the way. He again felt the rats' feet unraveling the cold knot of fear in his stomach.

"I'll let you know when you can go!" Calvin warned. "We got a few questions about that pretty mama of yours."

Why did they keep talking about Mama? Mama didn't bother anybody. She just stayed home and answered the telephone. If only . . . Harry looked up at Calvin.

"You better look out!" he cried, feeling the tears close under his eyelids. "Our daddy's gonna be here in a minute!" He looked at Henry, whose mouth opened in a round of surprise.

"Y'all ain't got no daddy," Arnold scoffed.

"We do too!" cried Harry desperately.

"He's a Flying Tiger!" Henry yelled, slamming his empty bottle down on the bar.

Crecencio reached for the bottle. "Come on," he said in a warning tone of voice, "Ju let t'em boys go." He tried to imagine his own son, Berto, sitting here on the bar talking to two no-good drunks like these, being asked questions about *his* dark-eyed mother. Theresa. Berto.

He took a step toward the bar.

Calvin turned on him suddenly. "You want your jaw broke?" he threatened.

Without warning, Henry kicked, hard, landing a foot right in Calvin's crotch. Calvin
doubled over, moaning.

Crecencio grinned, but Harry felt the fear
unroll itself into a living coil that filled his whole
body. No!

"You little sonofabitch," Calvin gasped, fas-
tening an eye of hatred on Henry. "You just
done the wrong thing!"

Arnold giggled at him.

"It ain't funny!" Calvin snapped.

Arnold quit laughing immediately, as Calvin
ripped loose his belt buckle and jerked the
heavy strip of leather through the beltloops.

Crecencio stepped toward him.

"I'm gonna tan your ass, little boy!" Calvin
snarled.

"No, you're not!" yelled a voice suddenly from
behind them.

Calvin and Arnold spun around.

"Teddy!" cried Harry, at the sight of the white
suit in the doorway.

"Well goddamn now, if it ain't the rest of the
U.S. Navy," giggled Arnold, appraising the
slight figure of the young sailor.

Calvin laughed too.

"Come on, boys," said Teddy. "It's time to go."

Harry pushed himself to the edge of the bar,
but Calvin shoved against his knees, pinning
him there.

"They ain't going nowhere," he said, "not till
they get some red marks on they ass."

"Come on, boys," Teddy repeated, calmly eyeing Calvin. "Get on down off the bar."

Arnold stepped in front of Henry.

"Looks like we got us some trouble," Calvin said to him.

"Looks like, don't it," Arnold smiled.

"You've had your fun," said Teddy.

"We ain't through," Arnold grinned. "Not by a damn sight."

"You're through," Teddy said, taking a step toward them.

"Admiral," Calvin leered, watching his approach, "you must have balls of steel, walking in here like this." He put down his beer bottle and pushed up his sleeves.

He'll hurt Teddy! Harry thought, and launched a mighty kick at Calvin's already-bruised balls of flesh. Once again, Calvin doubled over, gasping.

"Hey!" yelled Teddy, lunging for Arnold, who punched him hard in the stomach with his pool cue, knocking out his breath. But even as Teddy staggered and fell, Harry leaped like a Kamikaze from the bar onto Arnold's back, biting his ear and screaming.

Standing up on the bar, Harry watched Arnold whirl and bellow with Henry on his back.

Calvin straightened up and took a step toward Teddy, struggling to his feet.

With a leap, Harry clamped his legs around Calvin's middle and his hands over the startled man's eyes.

"Teddy!" he yelled. "Teddy!"

And Teddy punched Calvin four good ones to the stomach, sending him crashing to the floor. Harry jumped off into Teddy's arms like a rodeo rider who's gone to the buzzer.

Pushing Harry toward the door, Teddy reached for Henry, who still clung ferociously to Arnold's back. But Arnold, as soon as his ear was free from the clamp of Henry's jaws, swung at Teddy, socking him full in the face and knocking him to the floor once more.

"Teddy!" Harry grabbed Arnold's left leg and hung onto the evil-toed boot which was about to kick the sailor.

"Teddy!" Henry threw his weight onto Arnold's right leg and hung on as tightly as he could.

"Git off!" growled Arnold, kicking first his left leg into a chair trying to dislodge its passenger, and then his right leg into a table. The boys clung like leeches. Arnold stamped his feet up and down, pounding the boys against the floor like pile drivers, but still they hung on.

Finally he stopped his clog dance and leaned over, prying at the little fingers that had caught in his pants legs like claws. But Teddy, ready for this, caught him with a quick uppercut that sent him over backwards, a sack of feed that slumped against the bar.

Calvin had pulled himself painfully to his feet and now, very slowly, he opened a huge gleaming pocket knife. His eyes flashed meanly toward Teddy.

The sailor gasped, as the same rats' feet of fear Harry had felt began to clamber up *his* insides, trying to get away.

"No, Teddy!" cried Harry.

"Oh no!" yelled Crecencio. "No, no ju don't!" He pulled a shotgun from under the bar.

Calvin took a step toward Teddy, holding the knife low, his eyes glinting maliciously.

"Hey!" yelled Crecencio. "Ju better look what I got here!"

No one looked.

Teddy stepped back, raising his hand, as Calvin took another step toward him.

Ka-bloom!

The shotgun! A flurry of dust and green felt disintegrated the top of the pool table just to Calvin's left.

No one moved in the sudden silence.

"Next time it's gonna be jour brains up there on the ceiling!" yelled Crecencio, waving the shotgun toward Calvin.

Calvin whirled, slashing at the bartender with his knife. But quick as a fighting cock, the Mexican swung the shotgun at him, catching him across the temple with a heavy thud.

Calvin went down. His knife clattered to the floor beside him. He lay very still.

Crecencio sighed in the awed silence. "Aw, goddamn me! Ju take a look what I don to my pool table."

Teddy knelt down beside Harry and Henry, huddled under a table. "Y'all Okay?" he asked.

"We're Okay, Teddy!" Harry cried tearfully, flinging his arms around the sailor's neck.

"I'm kinda scared," said Henry, as Teddy hugged them both. He looked anxiously at the destroyed felt of the pool table.

"J'all better scoot before two locos t'ey wake up," Crecencio said.

"Thanks for the help," said Teddy. He took the boys' hands and turned toward the door.

"Aw naw," said the bartender. "That's Okay." He ran his hand sadly across the blasted green lawn of his pool table.

Calvin pushed himself painfully to his elbows and glared after the departing trio.

"Hey!" he called, sitting up and rubbing the bleeding cut in his cheek.

Teddy and the boys looked back.

"I wouldn't come around here no more if I was you, sailor boy," he said, real malice cutting through the throbbing pain in his voice.

"Ju chut up down there." Crecencio leaned over the bar with the shotgun still in his hand. "Or I give ju another clonk on jour head."

The last thing Harry saw as he followed Teddy and Henry out the door was the glint in Calvin's eye, as cold and sharp as the blade of the knife that still lay beside him on the dusty floor.

15

Teddy winced and tried to smile at Nita as she dabbed the bright orange dots of Merthiolate over the cuts on his face. She was still so frightened by their story of the fight that she was not smiling at all.

"You're gonna look polka-dotted, Teddy!" laughed Harry.

Henry giggled.

"You'd better hold still," said Nita, when Teddy smiled again. She recapped the bottle and sat down at the table, fixing a cold, parental stare on Henry and Harry.

"What in the world were y'all thinking, to go into a place like that?" she asked.

Harry squirmed guiltily and looked at Henry.

"I swear," she said. "I just can't get over it."

Henry and Harry both looked at the floor, waiting for the lecture to be over.

"Well," she concluded, "I hope y'all learned your lesson."

"We did, Mama," said Harry, relieved.

"We did, Mama," echoed Henry, nodding emphatically.

"Y'all sure!" she asked.

"Yes, ma'am," said Harry.

"Henry?" she demanded.

"Yes, ma'am," he nodded again.

She looked at them for a long moment. "Okay," she said, releasing them finally. "Y'all run on outside now."

"You coming, Teddy?" Henry asked, pushing back his chair.

"In a minute," he smiled. "Y'all run on."

The two boys headed for the front door as quickly as possible, lest Nita change her mind and decide to amend or add to her lecture.

Nita let out a long sigh. "This kinda thing scares me to death, Teddy," she said, as soon as the screen banged shut behind them. "They're just little boys."

"It was just a couple of drunks," said Teddy, trying to reassure her, "teasing around . . ."

"I wish I could get them outta here." Her voice was shaking. . . . "Someway . . ." The tears flooded her eyes.

"Nita . . ." he began, but she shook her head and reached for the bottle of Merthiolate.

Harry was pushing a wheelless toy truck around in the dust by the porch steps when Mr. Bailey stumbled into the yard with his lawn-mower.

"Hi, Mr. Bailey," he called. "Where you going?"

Mr. Bailey motioned up the road, but he

peered intently toward the door of the house.

"Gonna mow some grass?" Harry asked.

Before Mr. Bailey could finish nodding, Henry's feet swung in a rapid arc from the bottom limb of the chinaberry tree, landing with a thud in front of the lawn mower. Smiling, embarrassed again, he hitched up his overalls.

"Got time for a new game?" He tilted his blond face up toward Mr. Bailey.

Mr. Bailey nodded and stepped back from the handle of the lawnmower, squinting toward the screen again.

"What new game?" asked Harry, dropping the toy truck in the dust.

"Y'all follow me!" Henry ran around the corner of the house with Harry in close pursuit and Mr. Bailey shuffling behind.

"Maybe I oughta send them to my sister's where somebody could look after them," Nita was saying tearfully to Teddy. "Maybe I should. Maybe that'd be the best."

"You couldn't part with those boys," said Teddy, patting her hand. "You couldn't do that."

He was interrupted by a knock at the front door.

Nita looked up at him, puzzled, and then wiped her eyes. "I better go see who that is," she said, and stood up.

"Ma'am?" said the small narrow-shouldered man who stood on the front porch in a tight seersucker suit, wire-framed glasses, and a derby hat. "Mrs. Longley? Mrs. Nita Longley?"

"I'm Nita Longley," she nodded.

"Ma'am," he said through yellowed buck teeth, as he took off his hat. "I'm Gilstrap, Joe

Bill Gilstrap." He waited a moment for a response, but Nita only looked at him blankly. "Bailiff over at the county court," he added, pausing again.

"Yes, sir?" said Nita, puzzled but nodding.

"Yes, ma'am. Well, the Judge . . . " He looked up to see if that made an impression. "You know, he asked me to come over and look in on you. . . . "

"The Judge? The Judge! Oh! My letter!"

"Yes, ma'am. See how y'all are doing over here." He passed his hat from one hand to the other.

"Oh, yes sir!" cried Nita. "Oh, well, come in." She smoothed her dress and pushed open the screen.

"Yes, ma'am. Thank you."

As he stepped inside, she glanced quickly around the yard for the boys, but saw only Mr. Bailey's lawnmower under the chinaberry tree.

The faded red cattle truck with TRIPLETT BROTHERS LIGHT HAULING on the door clattered by on the road.

The Bailiff was standing in the front room, surveying the maroon couch.

"Is the Judge gonna help us?" Nita blurted, trying to straighten her hair.

"Never can tell about the Judge," said the Bailiff. "Asked me to make a report." He pulled a little notebook and a stubby pencil out of his pocket.

Nita nodded vaguely and wished she'd put on some lipstick. Report on what, she wondered.

"Let's see," he said. "You say you're frozen . . . in this job here?"

111

"Yes sir," said Nita, smiling as sweetly as she could. "That's the problem. I'm frozen. I can't even look for a better job. My boss—Mr. Rigby —says it's against the law."

"Yes, ma'am," he nodded officiously. "Well, you know there's a war going on."

"Yes, sir, I do know it," Nita folded her hands together demurely.

What was he supposed to write down? The Bailiff cleared his throat awkwardly. The Judge had just told him to take a look around with a sharp eye and a good ear. He took a look around.

"Everybody all over is gotta make sacrifices if we're gonna win this one," he said, putting his hat under his arm and striding across the room toward the corner beyond the pay phone to take another look around from over there.

"It ain't been going too well in some quarters, if you been listening to the radio here." He turned and eyed her, but the different vantage point gave him no new insights. He pretended to write something in his notebook, then glanced back at the radio and then at the what-not shelf above it.

"Yes, sir," Nita nodded nervously. "I know . . . But . . . "

"Even a high-up man like the Judge," he said, picking up the tin-framed photograph from the shelf, "he makes sacrifices."

"Yes, sir," said Nita anxiously, wondering what he had written. Why was he looking at the pictures?

"Husband?" he asked, squinting into the three gray-toned faces through his thick glasses.

"Yes," she nodded quickly, then, flustered, stammered, "I mean, no . . . that is . . . not any more. . . . " She looked at the floor.

"Divorced," he said curtly, shoving the picture back toward the shelf. He'd make a note of that, even though the Judge already knew it.

With a sudden clatter, the corner of the tin frame caught in the handle of the lacy white china basket, turning it over and spilling the tiny painted eggs onto the floor.

"No!" cried Nita.

The basket spun at the edge of the shelf and dropped, an empty nest, to shatter on the linoleum. A fragment of white china marked "State Fair" skittered under the couch. A piece of the delicate handle rolled to a stop at Nita's feet.

"My word," sniffed the Bailiff, trying to stand the photo upright. He stepped on a light blue egg, crushing it to a powder.

Nita dropped her hand limply to her side. The basket. Smashed.

"It's . . . Okay. . . ." she managed to say.

"Sorry . . ." he muttered, cursing the nervousness that had made him so clumsy, that had made him forget what he'd been saying.

Oh yes.

"Sacrifices!" he cried, suddenly rising up on his tiptoes in front of her, like a banty rooster flapping his wings.

Nita looked down at the eggs scattered about his feet.

"I make them too!" he cried. "Sacrifices. All the time. Somebody wants something these days, they gotta sacrifice."

Nita nodded again.

He picked his way out of the debris of egg shells and basket shards.

She looked scared. That was good, he thought.

"You live here, huh?" he said, glancing into the middle room. He was feeling more sure of himself again.

"Yes, sir," said Nita.

He wrote something in his notebook.

"Ain't a bad place," he pronounced as he looked around. "Not for a shotgun house, anyways. I've seen worse. The boys over in the Philippines don't have it this good, I bet. Mind if I take a look around?"

"No, sir," said Nita nervously, indicating the middle room doorway.

"Oh, hi," said the Bailiff, surprised to see Teddy still seated at the table. Judge had said divorcée, with two little kids. No husband, she said. Nobody'd mentioned a man around the place.

"Mosquito bites?" he asked, trying to cover his confusion.

Teddy blushed between the orange dots. "No, sir," he said awkwardly, as he stood up.

"Uh, how's the war going?" the Bailiff asked, shifting from one foot to the other. He pretended to consult his notebook.

"Just fine," Teddy nodded, smiling.

"Sure wish I could be over there with you boys," said the Bailiff, shaking his head and grinning through his buck teeth.

"Yes, sir," Teddy nodded. "I wish you could too."

"But I'm an officer of the court. You know how confining that is. A few of us got to keep

114

the home front going . . . the courts and so on.
We don't necessarily like it, but we gotta do it."
He shook his head emphatically once more.

"Yes, sir," Teddy nodded. "I understand."

"You give 'em a lick for me, Okay?" the Bailiff
grinned again, and cuffed Teddy on his sore
shoulder with a fist.

"Yes, sir," Teddy winced.

"Listen," the Bailiff went on, rocking back
on his heels. "How about painting my name on
one of them torpedoes? Gilstrap. G-I-L-
S-T-R-A-P. Joe Bill. Joe Bill Gilstrap." He smiled
effusively.

Teddy looked at him blankly.

"Uh, maybe you oughta write it down," said
the Bailiff. He spelled the name out on a page
from the notebook which he tore out and
handed to Teddy.

"G-I-L-S-T-R-A-P," Teddy read.

"That's it!" cried the Bailiff, cuffing him
again. He winked. "Shoot it to 'em! Make it
hurt!"

"Yes, sir," nodded Teddy, stepping back, just
out of range.

"I'd be much obliged," the Bailiff grinned, and
turned back toward Nita, who stood uncom-
fortably in the doorway.

"You're welcome," said Teddy. He sat down
again.

"Nice boy," the Bailiff said to Nita, notebook
and pencil poised once again. "Brother?"

"No, sir," Nita shook her head.

"Cousin, huh?" he smiled, ready to make the
notation.

"Well, no . . . " said Nita, fidgeting.

115

The Bailiff squinted at Teddy and then at Nita. A divorcée that didn't have no husband . . . well, who could this half-naked man be, sitting here all alone in the house with her? He tapped the end of his pencil against the notebook.

"You think the Judge'll help us?" Nita asked quickly, too quickly.

The Bailiff flicked his glance from Teddy to Nita without answering and finally made a notation in his notebook.

"I can tell you this much about the Judge," he said when he finished. "Number one, he believes in the war. He believes in sacrificing for it."

"Yes, sir," Nita nodded, trying to smile. "Well, you can see we're sacrificing. . . . "

"Yes, ma'am," he interrupted. "Number two: The Judge is Godfearing. He believes in God." He glanced at Teddy again.

"Yes, sir," Nita nodded frantically, and reached for her cross, pulling it out to be sure it was visible at the neck of her blouse. "Well, we do too."

"It's those two things, Number One and Number Two, that tell you what kind of man the Judge is. It's what this country was built on: the war and God!"

With that, he turned on his heel and headed for the front room, waving his forefinger in the air.

"Yes, sir . . . " Nita murmured as she trotted along behind.

"The Judge, he says, 'Goddamn the Japs!' 'Goddamn the Germans!'" The Bailiff was charging the front door. "I've heard him say it many times. Excuse the language." He had suddenly remembered that the Judge also believed in not offending ladies.

"Yes, sir," Nita stammered, feeling the crunch of a china fragment underfoot. "Well, thank you for coming out."

At the screen door he stopped and turned around, bowing slightly from the waist, with his hat under his arm and a gracious smile exposing his yellow incisors.

"That's all right. I like to use my influence to help people when I can. I better go file my report."

He raised his voice and yelled into the middle room. "Don't forget to give 'em a lick for old Joe Bill Gilstrap!"

"No, sir," Teddy called back from the middle room doorway. "I won't."

As the Bailiff stepped out onto the porch, Nita felt a wave of relief pass through her. That hadn't gone so badly, really, except for the basket. . . . Surely he'd file a favorable report. She smiled at him.

Suddenly from around the corner of the house she heard two familiar voices: "One, two, three, heil Hitler! One, two, three, heil Hitler!" She gasped in anguish.

The Bailiff peered curiously toward the chant which continued, growing louder each second, as it drew nearer. "One, two, three, heil Hitler! One, two, three, heil Hitler!"

No, thought Nita. No!

But there they were, goose-stepping joyfully around the corner of the porch, raising their right arms smartly in the Nazi salute: Harry and Henry and Mr. Bailey.

"Them ain't *your* boys?" the Bailiff said incredulously.

"Boys!" cried Nita frantically. "Boys! Stop that!"

Never hearing her, they continued to chant and giggle! "One, two, three, heil Hitler! One, two, three, heil Hitler!"

"They're walking like little German Nazis!" The Bailiff's voice rose in pitch as he stared, horrified and disbelieving.

"No!" Nita screamed in anguish. "Stop that! Stop that!"

Hearing her frantic voice, the boys stopped dead in their tracks and stared at the porch. What was that man doing to Mama that she wanted him to stop?

"It's a Jap!" bellowed Henry at the sight of the Bailiff's wire-rimmed glasses and buck teeth. "It's a Jap with Mama!"

"It's a Jap!" cried Harry.

Mr. Bailey grabbed in vain for their arms as the two boys dashed for the porch.

"Just meet them," Nita tried to smile at the Bailiff as the boys ran toward them. "They're good boys. I don't know where on earth they learned to walk like that . . . "

But before she could finish her sentence, Henry had bounded up the steps and plowed into the Bailiff's knees and Harry into his midsection, knocking the little man backwards off the end of the porch.

"What the. . . ? " gasped the Bailiff as he hit the dirt.

Nita put her hands over her eyes and wondered if she was going to faint.

"You dirty Jap!" cried Henry, as he threw clods of dirt at the Bailiff. "You leave Mama alone!"

"You dirty Jap!" Harry hit him in the middle of the forehead.

"Boys!" Nita yelled, suddenly overcome by anger. They had ruined everything, the only chance. "Stop it! Stop it!" She was aware of Teddy in the doorway behind her.

"What is this?" yelled the Bailiff, on his hands and knees, feeling around in the dust for his glasses. "I'm an officer of the court!"

A barrage of dirt clumps hit him on the rump.

"Boys!" Nita hollored.

Teddy jumped off the porch and grabbed Henry just as he let fly with another clod.

Pulling himself to his feet, the Bailiff dusted off his seersucker suit with his hat.

"This will go in my report," he said icily to Nita, as he hurried past Mr. Bailey to his car.

And so will that half-naked sailor boy, he huffed to himself as he climbed into the seat. This was exactly why it was so important to have an officer of the court come take a look around. The Judge sure knew his business, all right. Just because somebody writes a damn letter doesn't mean they're Godfearing, war-loving citizens like you'd expect!

Nita grabbed Harry's arm and shook it.

"Y'all get in the house!" she said furiously. "Get in the house right now!"

Harry looked alarmed but followed Henry and Teddy inside.

119

Nita turned on Mr. Bailey. "What did you think you were doing?" she cried in tears. "Teaching them to walk like that! Don't you come back around·here! Not ever!"

Mr. Bailey looked at the ground.

"Go on! Get away from here! You stay away from my boys! You hear me now? Go on!"

Sadly Mr. Bailey reached for the handle of his lawnmower and stumbled away down the road.

"There it went!" Nita yelled at Harry and Henry as she pulled open the front screen. "Our one chance!"

The boys and Teddy were sitting silently at the table in the middle room.

"Nita . . . " Teddy said gently.

"We're sorry, Mama," said Harry, frightened by her angry tears.

"Y'all mess up *everything!*" Nita yelled.

"We're sorry," said Henry, reaching for her hand, "honest, Mama."

"Walking like that!" Nita jerked his arm. "That . . . that raggedy man is never to come around here again! You hear me? Never!" She looked from one little face to the other. "Not ever!"

Henry began to cry. "Mama," he sniffled, "I showed Mr. Bailey how to walk like that."

"Mr. Bailey didn't do anything, Mama," said Harry, blinking back his own tears. He didn't understand what had happened. Why was Mama mad?

"They saw it in the newsreel, Nita," said Teddy quietly.

"I don't care where they got it . . . " she began angrily, but then dissolved in a new flood of tears. "Oh, Lord . . . " she gasped, sitting down and covering her face with her hands.

"Mama," said Harry tentatively, patting her hair. Why was she crying? He looked anxiously toward Teddy.

"My basket!" she sobbed. "He broke it. My egg basket!"

The egg basket? Harry bit his lip. Mama's egg basket was broken?

Henry pushed himself next to her and hugged her as tightly as he could.

When the switchboard buzzed, it was Henry who rushed to answer it while Nita wiped her eyes and tried to control her crying.

"The egg basket?" Harry asked fearfully.

"Hello?" Henry said, pushing in various cords and turning different switches. "Hello? This is Henry. Hello?"

The buzzing continued.

Wiping her eyes, Nita stood up and took the headset from Henry. "I'm all right now," she smiled at him.

"Number please?" she said into the headset. "Just a moment. I'll connect you."

Feeling almost as if he were dreaming, Harry looked through the doorway toward the shelf were the beautiful basket had always stood. Gone! He was terrified.

The debris was still scattered about the floor below. Just in front of his foot lay a little white fragment, curbed and sharp like the new moon.

He picked it up. It was not a dream.

Maybe it could be glued back. Maybe some of the eggs weren't broken. He squatted on the floor and began to pick up pieces. Yes, he would glue it back together.

Here was the green egg. He held it up—chipped but not broken.

Here were more pieces under the pay phone.

The dark red of his own blood surprised him at first. It smeared across a cool round piece of the yellow egg and then on a white splinter of the basket. Cut. A round drop fell to the floor under his finger. Funny how it didn't hurt.

Harry quickly stuck his cut finger in his mouth and stood up. He ran a toe through the shiny drop on the floor and then emptied the china fragments from his hand onto the shelf where the basket had stood next to the picture.

Mama's china basket of eggs was broken.

"Why don't you boys go on out and play now?" Teddy said quietly from the doorway.

Nita was still at the switchboard.

"Everything's okay," Teddy smiled, patting Harry on the shoulder and ruffling Henry's hair.

At the screen door, Harry glanced back toward the shelf again before he followed his younger brother out onto the porch. Broken! Putting his cut finger into his mouth, he tasted once again the secret knowledge of his own heart's dark blood.

"Nita . . . " Teddy began, after the boys had gone out.

"Oh, Teddy!" she sobbed. "I feel so caught . . . so trapped. . . . "

"I know." He put his arms around her and held her tight, her face buried against his shoulder, patting her the way a father would a hurt child.

"I'm sorry," she said after a minute, wiping her eyes. "I guess . . . I was really counting on some help from the Judge." She tried to smile at him but it didn't work.

"Nita . . . " he said softly again, patting her shoulder. "There's bound to be another way."

"No, there's not," she said, shaking her head emphatically. "We're stuck here, that's all."

The switchboard growled and flashed.

"Number please," she said.

"You could get married . . . " Teddy said.

"Just a moment. I'll connect you." She turned to Teddy with a surprised look. "Don't be silly," she said as she plugged in the cord.

"You could marry me," he said abruptly.

She glanced at him again, astonished.

"They couldn't keep you here then," he went on, frightened but determined. "We wouldn't have to stay married. You could decide later on."

Nita opened her mouth to speak, but he stumbled ahead.

"I know I'm younger. I know that might bother you . . . "

Nita's eyes filled with tears again, and still he blurted on.

"I'm shipping out in the morning. I'll be gone . . . "

Again came the raucous buzz.

"Number please," she said with difficulty. "Just a moment. I'll connect you."

She held out her hand to Teddy.

"No, Teddy," she said, choking on the words.

"We wouldn't have to live together," he said, squeezing her hand. "We . . . "

"No," she said firmly, feeling stronger than she had in weeks.

"It'd get you out of here!" he said desperately.

The switchboard buzzed again.

With a sudden fury, Nita turned to the machine and ripped out all the cords.

The buzzing continued.

"Where would it put you?" she cried.

"That wouldn't matter . . . " he said gently.

She stood up and turned to face him, tears in her eyes.

"It would to me!" she said fiercely, over the buzz of the switchboard. "It would to us!"

"I wanna do something, Nita," Teddy shrugged helplessly.

"Oh, Teddy, you have!" She put her arms around him and pulled him to her, her tears wetting his short blond hair. "You already have. It's been so long since anybody cared about me . . . about any of us. . . . "

She could feel his heart beating, feel his warm solidity, his young strength, his caring that had freed her from her trap.

They stood in the center of the room, their arms around each other, until the force of their quiet embrace stilled the buzz of the switchboard at last.

16

"It's ready." Harry held out the highly polished shoe to Teddy. "Look, you can see your face in it."

Glancing at Harry's shoe, Henry spit on the toe of the one he was working at and frantically rubbed it with the dirty cloth, working it into a dull smear. When another minute's rubbing didn't improve matters, he reluctantly handed it over to Teddy.

"They're sure gonna notice me, aren't they?" Teddy grinned, putting on his shoes and standing up to admire their mismatched splendor.

"Look at Mama!" Harry cried, as Nita came into the front room.

He had never seen her look so pretty: her dress all yellow and white flowers, starched and ironed, her hair more fluffy than usual, her eyes bigger and darker, her mouth smiling in a rosier smile.

"Hubba-hubba!" Henry giggled, staring in wonderment at her new incarnation.

Nita blushed and glanced at Teddy, whose warm and wordless smile said what she wanted to know. It had been so long since she'd gotten dressed up, put on makeup, worried her usually limp hair into curls and waves, she wasn't sure how to do it, wasn't confident the result was right.

Harry beamed and Henry giggled.

"You guys load this sea bag in the wagon," Teddy said, "I'll be out there in a minute."

With Harry pulling at the top and Henry pushing mightily at the bottom of the bag, together they wrestled it out the door and down the steps of the porch.

Teddy turned to Nita and found her smiling at him. How pretty she looked. . . .

"Well," he said sadly.

"Yeah," she smiled warmly.

"Here's my address," he said, fishing a piece of paper out of his pocket. "If you wanna write sometime . . . " He hadn't realized how hard it was going to be, saying goodbye. A week ago he hadn't even known them, and now . . .

Nita took the paper and looked at the numbers and letters on it.

"They got a way of getting the mail to the ship," he explained.

"Okay," she smiled, "You can write us here: Gregory, Texas. I don't think they'll have any trouble finding us." She laughed.

He nodded, then looked up into her eyes and smiled weakly. Kids and cows in a vacant lot. A woman in the doorway. The hollow ships

126

struck by the darkness of the towering waves. Anywhere, everywhere, any time, forevermore . . .

"Maybe some rainy night," he said, "you'll hear a knock on the door . . . and it'll be me standing there again. . . . "

Nita's eyes filled with tears. "Wouldn't that be something? . . . " she said softly, looking at the floor.

He pulled her into his arms. "I'm gonna miss y'all, Nita," he whispered into her fluffy hair. The words seemed to glide right past what he was really feeling without even touching it.

"We're gonna miss you too, Teddy." She pulled him closer. "It's been so nice . . . so nice . . . "

He closed his eyes and leaned his face into her hair, rocking slowly, letting the moment press its contours into the surface of his mind. It would have to last him a long, long time. . . .

The switchboard's buzzing pulled them apart.

With a resigned look, Nita squeezed his hand and, stepping through the door to the middle room, picked up the headset.

"Number please . . . "

Teddy stood alone by the couch. This was it. He was going, leaving home.

"Just a moment, please . . . I'll connect you."

How familiar it had all become in just a few days. He pushed open the screen door.

Harry and Henry were waiting in the wagon on top of the sea bag under the chinaberry tree.

"All ready?" Teddy asked them, stepping off the porch. He picked up the wagon's handle and looked around the yard for the last time: the bicycle, the chinaberry tree, the cow in the vacant lot across the road . . .

Harry nodded and Henry giggled.

Teddy turned to look toward the house once more.

"Bye, Nita," he called into the pink-glazed doorway.

"Good luck, Teddy," she called back from the middle room.

With a sigh, he pulled the wagon with its cargo of sea bag and boys across the yard to the road.

When they were halfway to the highway, Nita pushed open the front screen and watched their distant figures growing smaller with each step.

"Goodbye, Teddy," she whispered. When she looked down at her bright pretty skirt, the yellow and white flowers seemed to be floating on the surface of swirling water, drifting swiftly downstream in the eddies of her tears.

At the highway, Teddy pulled the wagon off to one side of the road and lifted Harry and Henry to the ground and knelt to hug them goodbye.

Harry stepped back stiffly.

"Why do you have to go?" he asked, a tinge of anger reddening his voice as he avoided the embrace.

He looked off down the highway. Why did they always leave, just when you wanted them to stay the most? Why was Teddy leaving, just like his daddy had left? Harry wanted to run away himself and never come back. He wanted to hit Teddy. He wanted to cry.

"Harry . . . " Teddy began, reaching a hand toward him.

"You don't *have* to go!" Harry interrupted, accusing. "You wanna go!"

"No, I don't!" Teddy protested, surprised by Harry's tone and angry glare.

"You could stay if you wanted to! You did the other night! You said you had to leave and then you stayed!"

"I want to stay now even more than I did then," said Teddy seriously. "But now my leave is up. I have to go or they'll put me in jail."

Harry blinked twice and then suddenly threw his arms around Teddy, sobbing.

Henry began to sniffle too.

Pushing back his own tears, Teddy hugged them both.

"It's gonna be all right," he whispered.

Squeezing Teddy's neck tightly, Harry rubbed his cheek against the close-shaven whiskers. Teddy's leaving. He thought of the shattered china basket.

"Know what I'm gonna do?" Teddy said, straightening up with a watery smile.

"What?" sniffed Harry, rubbing his nose.

Teddy tapped his dull shoe. "I'm gonna name this shoe Henry." He looked up at the younger boy and then tapped the shiny one. "And I'm gonna name this one Harry." He smiled at Harry.

Henry giggled.

"Henry and Harry?" repeated Harry.

"Yeah," Teddy grinned. "That way, wherever I go, it'll be . . ." He stood up and marched along the edge of the pavement, swinging his arms and clomping his feet in time. "Henry and Harry, Henry and Harry, right there with me." He marched back to them, "Henry and Harry, Henry and Harry," and put his arms around them. "Okay?" he asked.

"Okay," they said in unison.

He lifted his sea bag out of the wagon.

"Y'all take care of your mama."

"We will," said Harry. With a sigh he watched Teddy cross the highway.

"Henry and Harry," Teddy called back over his shoulder as he walked. "Henry and Harry!"

"Henry and Harry!" both boys joined in.

The very first car stopped in response to Teddy's stuck-out thumb.

None of them noticed the Triplett brothers' truck slow down as it passed by from the other direction.

"Don't let the Japs get you!" Henry shouted across the highway as Teddy stowed his sea bag in the back seat of the car.

Teddy nodded and waved, and then he was gone.

17

Harry closed the back door quietly and hung
the flashlight on its nail. Henry was already in the middle room where Nita was
pulling off her headset.

"Goodnight, Mama," said the younger boy.

"Goodnight." She leaned over to kiss him.

Harry lingered in the doorway.

"Mama . . . " he began tentatively after Henry
had scampered off to bed.

She looked up and smiled.

"Mama, why couldn't Teddy be our daddy?"
He looked to see if the question would make her
angry. "Henry and me really liked him . . . "

"I know, honey," she said, drawing him to
her. "I liked him too."

"He liked us, Mama."

Nita smoothed his hair. "Well, there's more
to being a daddy than just liking somebody,"
she said.

"Did our real daddy more than just like us?" He looked down at the floor.

Nita hesitated just a moment. "I'm sure he did," she said.

"Do you miss him, Mama?"

"Yes . . . " said Nita after another slight pause. "I miss him."

"Then why isn't he with us?" Harry stepped back, searching her face. Somewhere there must be answers to these questions.

"Sometimes grown-up people want different things out of life," she said. "It's hard to explain." What was it I wanted, she wondered.

"What'd you want, Mama?"

She looked at him and then let her glance wander away vaguely. "I guess I just wanted to be a homebody," she said, shrugging her shoulders.

"And Daddy?" he asked. "What'd he want?"

"He wanted to go places," she said softly.

Harry looked very sad. "Well," he said, "why didn't y'all just take turns?"

"I guess we never thought about it," she admitted. (It was Nita's turn to look at the floor.) "I wish we had." She tried to remember why it hadn't occurred to her that they could just take turns—the way she'd taught the boys. . . .

She kissed him again. "You get some sleep now."

At the bedroom door he turned to her once more.

"Mama, where *is* our daddy?"

"I don't know, honey," she said. "He joined the Army when the war started. That was the last I heard."

"You think he still loves us?"

Nita smiled. "Your daddy wasn't the kinda daddy who could stop loving his boys."

"He'd be here if he loved us," Harry said emphatically, as he disappeared into the bedroom.

"Harry," she called, feeling very tired. "Honey, don't worry so much . . . " She ran a hand through her damp hair.

There was a long pause.

"Goodnight, Mama," he answered from the bedroom.

After a few minutes, Nita got up tiredly and pulled the door to the back room closed. There was no one here now but herself and the switchboard.

There was no one asleep on the front room couch. Teddy was gone. She walked slowly through the room and stopped at the whatnot shelf in the corner. The photograph stood there in its dull tin frame. Harry and Henry and Walter all looking so happy.

Beside the picture lay the little heap of china fragments. State Fair of Texas, 1934.

Nita began to cry, very quietly, all alone.

18

Mr. Rigby was whistling when he got out of the Southwestern Consolidated Telephone Company car the next morning. From his perch in the chinaberry tree, Henry watched closely. A tall woman, her hair piled over her forehead in stringy ringlets, got out of the car and followed Mr. Rigby's dark suit on her skinny legs.

"Well, hello there, Henry," Mr. Rigby called jovially to the brown feet above his head. "Catching any Japs?"

"I thought I had me one yesterday," said Henry, peering down at them.

The lady squinted up.

"That right?" said Mr. Rigby. "Well, you keep looking. You're doing a real service for the country. Ever'body's real proud of you."

"This here's Miss Andrews." He indicated the skinny woman whose bright red painted

134

mouth, Henry now noticed, far extended the edges of her real lips.

"Hi, Miss Andrews," he said.

"What'd he say you're doing up in that tree?" the woman called to him.

"Well, I was watching for Japs in submarines," said Henry. "But I think they're mostly in airplanes. Do you know what they look like?" He wanted to tell her they didn't look a thing like the cartoon in his overalls pocket.

"Say yes," he heard Mr. Rigby whisper to her.

"Yeah, I know what they look like," she called. "They're skinny little bastards."

Mr. Rigby grabbed her hand and pulled her toward the porch.

"And they're mean," Henry called, "and they try to shoot you, but sometimes they get shot." He wanted to explain to her all his newly gained knowledge on this subject.

"Keep up the good work, Henry," said Mr. Rigby cheerfully.

"Don't start no damn conversation," he hissed to Miss Andrews.

Around the corner of the house came Harry, wobbling on the old blue bike.

"Looking good, Harry," beamed Mr. Rigby, pulling Miss Andrews out of harm's way. "You're getting it."

Surprised, Harry looked up and, as Henry watched between his bare feet, the wavering bike turned over in a heap, pitching Harry in the dust.

"Nita!" called the cheerful Mr. Rigby through the screen, as he pulled off his straw hat. "Hello! John Rigby here!"

He ushered Miss Andrews into the hot, rosy front room.

"Oh good," he smiled broadly when Nita appeared at the door to the middle room. "You're here!"

"Where'd you think I'd be?" Nita asked suspiciously.

"This is Miss Andrews, Nita," he smiled, bowing slightly. "Miss Andrews, this is Nita Longley."

"Hello," said Nita.

"Jesus, what a dump!" sniffed Miss Andrews, the wide corners of her bright red mouth turning down as she surveyed the sagging couch and the Pepto-Bismol-colored walls.

"Nita," said Mr. Rigby quickly. "I got some good news, something I been working on for a long time. It just came through this morning."

"Hey, Johnny Boy," interrupted Miss Andrews, "this ain't exactly the way you described it."

"I couldn't tell you before now," he went on, throwing a warning glance at Miss Andrews, "because I was afraid it'd hurt your feelings if it didn't work out, but . . . "

"I ain't living in this kinda shit!" Miss Andrews snapped, stamping one of her skinny feet.

"This morning I got the good news I been working for. Yes, even praying for," Mr. Rigby beamed. "Nita, I got you a transfer."

"You *what*?" cried Nita.

"It's a surprise to me too, honey!" said Miss Andrews, folding her arms across her chest.

136

"Wichita Falls!" he grinned. "Nice office, regular hours. Miss Andrews is replacing you here."

"Don't be too sure, bub!" said Miss Andrews, pulling a cigarette from a case in her purse and lighting it.

"You'll be chief operator," Mr. Rigby rushed on. "How does that sound? Three other girls in the office. You'll have a desk, eight to five. Course you'll be making more money . . . "

"Mr. Rigby?" Nita covered her mouth with her hand in disbelief.

"Here, look!" He reached into his coat pocket. "Bus tickets for you and the boys. I bought 'em myself, right outta my own pocket."

"Mr. Rigby, if you're fooling . . . " said Nita weakly, fingering the cross at her throat.

"Bus leaves in the morning." He handed her the tickets. "See? Time's on the ticket."

"Ten o'clock?" Nita read.

"That's right, ten o'clock!" he cried, extending his hand to shake hers. "*Congratulations, Nita!*"

Leaning against the doorway, Nita was still looking blankly at the tickets as Mr. Rigby grabbed Miss Andrews' arm and wheeled her toward the door in a cloud of cigarette smoke.

"I hate to run," he said, "but we gotta get on back to the main office, get Miss Andrews' papers all filled out."

"We may have to renegotiate our deal, Johnny Boy," Miss Andrews snorted, with a wide red grimace.

Pushing open the front screen, Mr. Rigby

stopped dead still and exhaled like a punctured balloon, as a gray Ford pulled up behind his car on the road.

"Oh, oh!" he murmured.

Parting the chinaberry leaves, Henry watched the car roll to a stop and saw the driver's door open. It was the same man with the buck teeth and glasses who was here before —the Jap that had talked to Mama, the one she had gotten so mad about! Henry drew up his feet to make himself less visible and watched the man as he walked around the car and opened the back door. Another man was climbing out.

Then the Jap got back in the car while the other man walked toward the house. Henry leaned over, almost lying on the branch. Maybe it was a trick.

"Halt, mister!" he bellowed in a sinister voice.

The man below stopped in the middle of the yard and looked around in all directions.

"Who are you and whatta you want?" Henry demanded.

The man looked up.

"Dudley!"

The man smiled. "Hello, Henry."

The man from the bus, Dudley Voss! Excitedly, Henry started climbing down from the tree, forgetting for a moment that Dudley had gotten out of the car the Jap was still in.

"I thought I might be seeing you today," said Dudley, as Henry swung below the branch and dropped in a heap in the dirt.

"What're you doing here, Dudley?" Henry

asked, jumping to his feet and brushing off the dirt.

"I got a little bidness with your mama," Dudley smiled, "and with that man there." He glared toward Mr. Rigby, still standing in the doorway, flanked by Miss Andrews and Nita.

"Mrs. Longley?" Dudley said, stepping up on the porch. "I'm Judge Voss."

"Dudley!" cried Henry. "You a judge?"

"Henry!" said Nita.

"It's all right," Judge Voss smiled. "We're old friends."

Mr. Rigby tried to edge his way past him and down the steps.

"You John Rigby?" Judge Voss asked. "You beat it right on over here, didn't you?"

Mr. Rigby gulped and glanced at Nita.

Miss Andrews exhaled a long stream of cigarette smoke. Henry watched from the bottom step.

"What'd he tell you, Mrs. Longley?" the Judge asked.

"That I got a transfer," said Nita. "Wichita Falls . . ."

"I'd been working on it a long time, Judge," Mr. Rigby stammered. "I . . . "

"He tell you he's been lying to you?" Judge Voss demanded.

"Oh, oh," sneered Miss Andrews, tossing her red-stained cigarette into the dusty yard. "Johnny Boy's in trouble!"

Mr. Rigby frowned at the porch floor.

"No, sir . . . " said Nita, looking from one man to the other in confusion.

"He tell you you aren't frozen, never have been frozen?" the Judge demanded, folding his arms and glaring at Mr. Rigby, who seemed to be melting into a dark-suited puddle. "He tell you that under the law you haven't been making enough money to be frozen in this job?"

"No, sir," Nita stared at him in disbelief. "He didn't tell me that."

"Well, that's the truth of it," he said. "I checked with the Agency myself. It's cut and dried. Under the law you're simply not making enough money to be frozen."

"I got you a replacement, Nita," said Mr. Rigby desperately. "I did that."

"It ain't gonna be me, buster," growled Miss Andrews.

"I called his company this morning," said the Judge. "They didn't know anything about all this. They arranged the transfer to Wichita Falls."

"And, ma'am," he said to Miss Andrews, "they've already found a replacement for this office.

"Where?" she scoffed. "At the state insane aslyum?"

"They did?" asked Mr. Rigby in surprise. "Who?"

"The company decided on you, Mr. Rigby," Judge Voss smiled.

"Me?" he gasped. "I'll quit!"

"And break the law?" said the Judge. "You're frozen! *You are* making enough money to be frozen here till the war's over."

Helplessly, Mr. Rigby looked from Judge Voss to Nita to Miss Andrews.

"They want to see you at the main office," said the Judge.

"Ain't that something!" laughed Miss Andrews. "Mister Big Time's gonna be a telephone operator!"

Glaring at her, Mr. Rigby turned on his pudgy heel and walked rapidly toward his car.

Miss Andrews sauntered after him, swinging her purse and laughing.

Nita leaned weakly against the 2 x 4 post. Wichita Falls!

As Harry wobbled up on the bike, Henry leaped off the step into the yard.

"We're moving!" she yelled.

With a startled twitch of the handlebar, the bike crumpled to the ground. When the dust had cleared, Harry was running toward the porch like a character from an animated cartoon.

Moving?

"Well, I sure thank you," Nita smiled at Judge Voss. "I thought we'd lost our chance yesterday."

"You mean when my Bailiff was over here?"

She nodded.

Henry laughed. "Harry and me thought he was a Jap, didn't we, Harry?"

Embarrassed, Harry glanced at the Judge, then at the Bailiff sitting in the car, and then at his shoes.

"He told me," the Judge chuckled. "He ain't over it yet!"

He turned to Nita. "I was planning to look into your situation a little deeper anyway," he said. "Then your friend kinda hurried me up."

"What friend?" she asked.

"That sailor boy . . . I forget his name . . . "

"Oh," she smiled. "Teddy!"

"That's right," he nodded. "Teddy, I believe it was. He came by last night. Told me how things were over here."

She grinned. Teddy!

The switchboard buzzed.

"Good luck with the new job," the Judge said, extending his hand.

Nita shook it.

"Thanks . . . for everything, Judge. It means so much to us. . . . "

His eyes were warm and gray.

She pulled open the screen and disappeared into the pinkness to answer the switchboard's call.

"Well, boys . . . " said the Judge, extending his hand to Harry, who solemnly shook it.

"You write me a letter some time," he said to Henry, as he shook his hand.

"I can't write yet," said Henry, embarrassed. "But I can draw."

"That'll be fine. You send me a picture," the Judge grinned, as he stepped off the porch and walked toward his car and the waiting Bailiff.

"I'll send you a picture of a flying tiger!" Henry called. "But, you know," he added, "it's not really a tiger!"

The Judge smiled and waved as the Bailiff opened the door for him and he climbed into the car.

"Joe Bill . . . " said the Judge quietly, when the Bailiff had gotten back behind the wheel and pulled the car onto the road.

"Yes sir, Judge?"

"I wanta tell you something, Joe Bill." He slipped the paper and band off a new cigar. "Something important."

"Yes sir, Judge," said the Bailiff eagerly.

The Judge bit off the end of the cigar and lit it.

"Joe Bill, you are about the worst judge of human character I ever saw."

"Yes sir, Judge," the Bailiff murmured.

A huge cloud of cigar smoke settled over him.

19

Henry crouched with his elbows on the cracked linoleum of the kitchen floor and his chin in his hands, reading the colored drawing of the funny papers. The Katzenjammer Kids were being chased by a large dog with a spikey collar that matched his teeth. Henry giggled.

"Here," said Harry, lifting the last two cups off their hooks and holding them out to the younger boy.

"Will they have comics in Wichita Falls?" Henry asked, wrapping the running figures of Hans and Fritz around the cup and shoving the colorful wad into the cardboard box by the table.

"I don't know," said Harry. "I guess so." He pulled a chair over to the drainboard and climbed up on it to reach the higher shelves.

Before wrapping the other cup, Henry looked carefully at the pictures in "Terry and the Pi-

144

rates" for drawings of the mustard-yellow figures he had learned were Japs. But there were none.

He wondered if people in Wichita Falls knew about Japs. He wondered if they knew that people could get shot like birds and fall down cold and dead, hurt too bad to wake up again, kilt . . .

"Here, Henry," said Harry, lowering the clear pressed glass sugar bowl from its niche on the top shelf.

The sugar bowl! Henry jumped up and took the dish from his brother.

As soon as Harry turned back to the cupboard, Henry slipped off the lid and scooped out a handful of the grainy sweetness to stuff into his mouth as fast as he could.

"Caught you!" Nita laughed, peeking around the door as Henry licked the last of the white crystals off his sticky fingers.

She reached for him playfully, but Henry squealed and, giggling, dived under the table, scattering newspapers behind him.

"Come on, Harry!" Nita dropped to all fours and crawled under the table after Henry. "Let's get him!"

With a whoop, Harry climbed down off the drainboard and grabbed at his brother's overall legs, while Nita tickled him and Henry kicked and squealed, "Stop! Stop!"

When Nita fell back laughing and gasping for breath, Harry and Henry together turned on her, tickling and giggling.

"Oh, Harry!" she laughed, "Henry! Oh! Oh!" Grabbing them both, one in each arm, she pulled them to her, holding them close so that they all three lay laughing amid the crumpled witness of Nancy and Sluggo and square-jawed Dick Tracy, on the kitchen floor under the metal table.

Henry couldn't remember his mother playing with them like this before. But it didn't seem strange. It felt good.

"Mama . . . " Harry asked after a minute, "are we really moving?"

"I guess we are," she grinned, squeezing him.

"But . . . " he started, "I've been wondering . . . "

Henry noted the worry in his brother's voice.

"But . . . how is our daddy gonna find us?" Harry blurted out.

Henry hadn't thought about that.

Nita squeezed them both again and kissed the top of Harry's head.

"Maybe someday we'll find us a new daddy," she said.

"You think so?" Harry's voice was doubtful.

Henry understood why. Getting a new daddy didn't seem to very easy. He thought of Teddy.

Closing her eyes, Nita rocked them both.

"We might," she whispered.

Harry and Henry both lay quietly, staring up at the underside of the table top with the soft strength of her arms around them.

"We-e-e'll make a wish up-on a sta-a-ar . . . " she sang softly into Harry's ear.

Two hours later the boys found Mr. Bailey pushing his lawn mower down the road.

"Guess what, Mr. Bailey!" cried Henry, as they dashed up.

Mr. Bailey squatted at the edge of the pavement and smiled his half-smile, shrugging his shoulders and looking from one boy to the other.

"We're moving!" Harry beamed. "Mama's gonna have a different job!"

Half of Mr. Bailey's face registered sharp surprise.

"We're moving to Wichita Falls," crowed Henry. "Know where that is, Mr. Bailey?"

Mr. Bailey raised a slow finger and pointed up the road to the north.

"A long way?" asked Harry sadly.

Mr. Bailey nodded, his eyes on Harry's face.

A long way?! With sudden realization, Henry looked from one to the other. Mr. Bailey!

"Can't you come too?" he asked.

Looking at the ground, Mr. Bailey shook his head no.

"But you could come see us some time," Harry pleaded, laying his hand on the handyman's arm. "Please?"

"Don't they have yards in Wichita Falls?" Henry asked, as the thought of life without Mr. Bailey tried to form itself in his mind. His lip trembled.

Mr. Bailey nodded yes, and blinked back the tears in his one good eye. He patted Henry on the head.

"We're leaving in the morning," said Harry with difficulty. He couldn't imagine never seeing Mr. Bailey again.

Pushing himself laboriously to his feet, Mr. Bailey stood up, wiped his eye, and began to rummage in the pocket of his tattered overalls.

147

He pulled out a gold Masonic ring, the scrolly insignia nearly rubbed smooth where it was set in the dark red stone. He handed the ring to Harry.

"You mean to keep?" Harry asked excitedly, as he examined the ring.

"Wow!" cried Henry. A real ring!

Nodding, Mr. Bailey motioned to both Harry and Henry.

"It's for me, too?" said Henry excitedly, reaching for the ring. Red and gold.

Mr. Bailey nodded again and then lifted his finger to his lips.

"Don't tell anybody about it?" said Henry.

Again, Mr. Bailey nodded.

Harry took the ring from Henry and stuck it in his pocket.

"We won't!" he said, excited too. "It'll be our secret!"

Mr. Bailey pulled both boys to him in a big hug.

"We're gonna miss you, Mr. Bailey!" Harry was near tears as he hugged Mr. Bailey's waist. "I think you're the best friend Henry and me ever had."

With tears falling down one cheek, Mr. Bailey motioned toward their home, telling them wordlessly to run along.

"I hope you come soon, Mr. Bailey!" called Henry, smiling. He was sure Mr. Bailey wouldn't have given them the ring if he hadn't intended to see them in Wichita Falls.

Mr. Bailey nodded and waved.

"Bye, Mr. Bailey," said Harry sadly, feeling the lump the ring made in his pocket and in his throat. Wichita Falls was a long ways away. Mr. Bailey would never come to visit, he knew.

The handyman turned back toward his lawn-mower, making himself busy with it until the sounds of the boys had diminished into the distance. Then he turned back, looking after them and beyond them to their shotgun house, half of his face lined deeply in mute sadness.

20

Nita turned from the front screen and looked through the house and out the back door. It was hard to realize they were leaving, and yet, there were the boxes stacked next to the door in the middle room.

She put her hand in the pocket of her house dress. And here were the bus tickets. Gregory to Wichita Falls. Ten A.M., she read in the late afternoon pink light of the front room.

The couch, the chair—she inventoried the room's contents. They'd leave the furniture behind. The round-topped radio, the whatnot shelf . . . she stopped. There was the photograph in its tin frame.

It could go in the middle of the pasteboard suitcase between her clothes, where the glass wouldn't get broken.

As she picked up the picture, she noticed the little pile of broken china.

1934. There was a curved fragment that had been the blue egg. Almost ten years. There had been nothing to do but to go on.

With the edge of the picture frame, she gently brushed the pieces of the basket and its contents into her hand. A part of her would be staying here.

This was the end of something, she felt. Of what? Of the helplessness, the hopelessness she had come to call her own?

Clutching the shards, she walked through the middle room to the back room and pushed open the back screen. Here in the late shadow by the steps she would bury it, this decade, this bit of the irrevocable past, now gone forever. . . .

With a stick she scratched a hole in the dust and dropped the remains of the basket into it. Things were going to be very different, she felt, from now on. When the dirt was pushed back over it, you couldn't even tell there had been a hole. She laid the stick across the spot.

Standing up, she brushed the dust off her hands and climbed the steps. The sun was going down, fading, receding. It rested on the horizon like a golden egg, momentary, ephemeral. She could see into the back room, through the door into the middle room, through the next door into the front room, and out the front door onto the porch still lit by the waning light.

With one hand on the screen, she turned and looked into the back yard once more, with

the overpowering feeling that she was on board
the back platform of the last car of a train, a
train pulling out of the depot, heading into the
gathering darkness heading for who knew
where, leaving all of this far behind.

21

Late that night, after Harry and Henry were in their beds on the other side of town, no one saw Calvin and Arnold's faded red cattle truck speeding down the dirt road on the far side of the cluster of Gregory's lights.

No one heard Calvin holler, "Here we go, Arnold!" And no one heard Arnold's insane giggle or saw the beer bottle fly out of the truck's window to crash against the roadside mailbox.

No one saw the truck's lights slow in front of a small farmhouse or heard the grinding of gears as Calvin shifted into low.

Only one person, startled awake in the darkened house by the bone-jarring crash as the truck rammed the front door, splintering the wall, engine roaring and spinning tires tearing madly at the plank steps, recognized the voices that yelled, "Wake up there, Pancho Villa!" and giggled, "Wake up! Wake up!"

Crecencio, alarmed, leaped out of bed in his underwear and listened with pounding heart to the honking truck horn's craven.

"*Por dios!* Crecencio! *Que pasa?*" cried Teresa, his wife, as the honking continued, insanely ripping the night. "Crecencio!"

In the other room, the kids began to wail. "Daddy!" he heard his son, Berto, call over the noise of the engine.

The light from the truck's headlights glared through the splintered wall of the living room, spotlighting the Virgin of Guadalupe who hung there helplessly in her gilt frame.

Crecencio raised his arm against the blinding glare. "Hey, stop that!" he called. "Hey, what ju doing?"

"Git 'im, Arnold!" he heard Calvin yell.

"Daddy!"

Those crazies!

Terrified, Crecencio ran from the light-flooded room toward the back door.

"Crecencio!" Teresa stood in the bedroom doorway, clutching a sheet in front of her.

The children! She ran to their room. Maria del Socorro and Adriana clung to each other, bawling, in the bed. Berto stood by the door, whimpering.

"Mama, what's happening?" he cried.

Fumbling with the hook on the door, terrified, she finally managed to latch it behind her.

Wiping away her own frightened tears, she grabbed the boy and pulled him to the bed with his sisters.

"It's Okay," she whispered. "Daddy's taking

care of it." Trembling, she hugged the three little bodies to her bosom.

They heard the back door slam and they listened as running footsteps passed by the window heading for the back yard from the front porch.

Outside, Crecencio was aware only of his breath ripping through his throat and his belly heaving as he sprinted across the open field behind his house. On the dry grass behind him him he heard the heavy footfalls of boots. No!

"Sic 'im!" he heard Calvin holler. "Sic 'im, Arnold!"

And as he stumbled, breathing heavily, into the barbed-wire fence at the edge of the field, Crecencio could hear Arnold's whooping giggle drawing closer, the way a big coon hound closes in on his quarry.

Berto . . . was the last thing he thought as he clawed at the barbed wire, trying to get through it.

He never even saw the piece of 2 x 4 that split open his head from behind, dropping him heavily, unbreathing, only his legs twitching in insensible spasms, onto the weed-grown fence's bottom strand.

22

B y the faint glow from the light above the switchboard in the middle room, Henry could make out from his bed the shapes of the cardboard box he and Harry had packed their toys in and the tin suitcase they had stuffed full of their overalls and bluejeans and underwear and tennis shoes, and of course their sailor suits.

Tomorrow they were going! Tomorrow they would leave here forever! It was exciting but also a little scary and a little sad. This was the last night he would sleep in his bed in his room. He couldn't remember ever having slept anywhere else.

This might be the last time he would go to the privy, he thought, as he padded across the floor to the nail where the flashlight hung by the back door. Turning, he looked through the doorway to the middle room, but Mama was sleeping soundly on her cot, with a stack of boxes and two old suitcases tied with rope beside the door to the front room.

The last time!

Halfway across the yard from the closed back door, he stepped on a sticker. The last time for a sticker in the back yard, he thought, as he pulled it out, with an audible "Ouch!"

Inside the privy with the door open behind him, he checked with his flashlights for spiders in the hole for the last time. He was reaching for the stick in the corner when a noise behind him made him turn in time to see the privy door swing shut.

"Hey!" he yelled, hearing the latch hooked from the outside. Was it Harry playing a trick on him? "Harry!" he bellowed.

There was no answer but that of the cicadas screaming in the vacant lot.

When the switchboard buzzed inside at that moment, Nita stirred and then sat up in the blinking light.

"Number please . . ." she murmured sleepily, pushing back the hair from her damp forehead.

A glance into the vacant lot would have shown her only the munching cow obscured by the brush under the cicadas' scream. Mr. Bailey had already ended his lonely, longing vigil.

But the same glance would have shown her two other figures just outside the circle of the porch light. The fatter one carried a full gunny sack into the shadows around the side of the house, while the taller, thinner one approached the porch.

Nita had just lain down on her cot again when she heard a soft knock at the front door. She pulled on her blue robe.

"Yes?" she said, opening the door the narrow crack the chain-lock allowed and feeling the cool breeze on her forehead.

"Ma'am," mumbled the figure on the porch, his hat pulled down over his face, "sorry to be bothering you this time of night. But I'm broke down out on the highway and I need to call my brother to come get me."

Nita squinted at the section of his face she could see between the hat and his upturned collar.

"Ma'am," he went on, "there just ain't another place in town open where I can get to a telephone."

"Well . . ." said Nita reluctantly. With a sigh, she realized that after tonight she wouldn't have to put up with this kind of thing anymore.

"Please, ma'am," he said. "I don't wanna have to sleep out there on the side of the highway all night."

"Well," she said sleepily. "All right." She pushed the door to and unlatched the chain.

"The pay phone's on the wall in here."

"Yes, ma'am," he said, stepping into the front room. "Thank you, ma'am."

"Just give me a second now," she said, as she went into the middle room.

"Yes, ma'am, I will," he said.

Nita pulled the door shut behind her and sat down at the switchboard. She opened the key.

"Number please?" she said.

But there was no answer. Hot and still, except for his breathing over the wire.

"Do you have the number?" she asked tiredly.

"No, ma'am," she heard through the headset and through the wall as well. "I got just about everything else I need, but a number—now, that's something I ain't got, sure enough."

"What's the name then?" she asked, a little irritated. "I'll have to look it up."

"Name's Johnny Mack Brown," he said, and giggled.

"Sir?" she asked, not recognizing the name and beginning to feel a little uneasy.

"Johnny Mack Brown," he repeated. "Ask me again and I'll knock you down!" A thin laugh came through the wire and the wall and stopped Nita's blood.

"I . . . I'm sorry," she finally managed to say. "I don't have a listing under that name."

Her mind was turning the rhyme over and over, nonsensically, Brown-down, down-Brown.

"You don't?" he laughed. "Well, I'll be damned."

Nita's fingers fumbled to the cross at her throat.

"Please . . ." she stammered, "I've got two little boys . . ." Brown-down.

"Yes, ma'am," he laughed. "Well, I already know your two boys."

"The poolhall . . ." she murmured. Fear had pressed to her chair. Down-Brown.

"Well, yes ma'am. That's where I met 'em," he said. "Yes ma'am. Sure is . . ."

"My friend's here, too," she whispered. "You must know . . ." Her eyes darted to the hook by the door.

"The sailor boy?" Calvin laughed. "No ma'am, he's not here. He's gone."

Pulling off her headset with shaking fingers, Nita pushed the chair back as quietly as she could and tiptoed to the door she had closed between herself and the front room. Browndown. If she could just latch . . .

But the door flew open under her hand and Calvin stood there, grinning nastily through his bruises from the fight and the long ugly gash Crecencio had opened in his cheek with the shotgun barrel.

He lifted his long hunting knife.

"Please," Nita cried, tears spilling down her cheeks, "my boys . . ."

"Tell you what, ma'am," he said, pushing her aside as he entered the room. "You don't give me no trouble and I sure won't give your boys no trouble. I'll make that deal with you."

Nita stood sobbing, her back to the stack of boxes, as Calvin cut the large tangle of wires at the base of the switchboard.

He glanced into the back room, but there was no movement in the boys' beds.

"Get on in there," he said, motioning toward the front room with the knife.

Clutching the cross in one hand and the front of her robe with the other, Nita shuffled fearfully into the front room.

"Get 'em off!" he barked from behind her.

So that was what he wanted.

Without turning around, she unbuttoned her

robe and let it fall to the floor. She was crying quietly.

"Turn around!" he demanded.

Down-around. Obediently she turned to face him, but she couldn't look at him.

With a growl, he motioned toward her with the knife.

Her breath shuddering, she slowly pushed the slip straps off her shoulders and let the light garment fall to her waist. One hand fluttered to the cross in a meager attempt to cover her breasts from his eyes. She couldn't stop her teeth from chattering.

"Hold it!" he yelled.

She dropped both hands to her sides and felt her hair wet against her cheeks, her body open, helpless, to his view.

"Make 'em bounce!" he hissed.

Nita didn't move. She couldn't even lift her eyes from the floor.

"Make 'em bounce!" he said again, his voice tight, his eyes glinting like knife-thrusts at her breasts.

Slowly, with the slip straps dangling-wrong-side out over her hips, Nita raised herself like a mechanical doll onto the balls of her feet and then lowered her weight onto her heels again.

Giggling he jabbed the knife at her. "Again!"

Again, she raised herself on her toes and then dropped back flatfooted. She felt like a stick figure, a crudely drawn cartoon in black and white. Down-around-Brown.

"Hey!" he called excitedly toward the window, still giggling. "Pssst! Arnold!"

"Yeah?" came a voice from out by the side of the house.

"How you doing out there?"

"I'm all ready."

"Get on in here then. I don't want you to miss the show!" Calvin called.

There was no response.

"The *show!*" Arnold called back excitedly.

At the sound of the second voice, it was all Nita could do to keep from bolting. Two of them! But she clung desperately to Calvin's promise: "You don't give me no trouble and I sure won't give your boys no trouble."

She could feel the sweat running down the inside of her arms and between her breasts.

Outside, hearing a footstep behind him, Arnold looked up from the pile of newspapers and kindling he was stacking in a mound against the house. As he started to stand, he heard the whooshing sound, as of a great sharp-taloned night-bird beating toward him on iron wings. That sound was the last fragment of his awareness.

The long-handled garden rake caught him full in the face, its steel prongs ripping into his flesh like the bloody beak of a cat-eyed raptor.

Inside, both Nita and Calvin heard it—a series of vicious noises, a gasp and a moan, ending with the sound of something heavy falling against the side of the house under the window. Then all was silence, but for Nita's ragged breath and the cicadas in the hot night.

Calvin listened intently and then stepped to the open window. "Hey!" he whispered loudly. "Hey, Arnold!"

There was no response.

"Hey!" he called louder. "Psssst! Hey!"

Still no answer.

Holding her breath, Nita listened with Calvin.

Alarm spreading across his face, Calvin stepped to the front door. Knife in hand, he opened the door slowly, and then, still holding the inside knob, stepped out onto the porch.

"Arnold?" he called.

Now! Nita threw her weight against the door, and heard the bones in Calvin's wrist crunch and snap. With an animal scream of pain, Calvin jerked his arm from the door, and Nita slammed it shut and locked it. She could hear him fall, groaning, from the porch to the ground.

Taking a deep breath, she ran to the middle room, feeling for the shotgun she had hidden behind the switchboard. Where was it? There! Her hand closed around it.

Breathing heavily, she dashed back to the front room. The light! She switched it off and pulled shut the door to the lighted middle room. Safer now in the full darkness, she grabbed her robe off the floor and yanked it around her trembling shoulders.

The shotgun was heavy in her hand.

In the darkened silence, she heard Calvin's voice from outside, full of pain: "Who's that? Who's that out there?"

She could hear no reply but her own gasping breath.

Then a sudden scream and the sounds of a struggle. A muffled moan and then nothing.

Listening with what felt like every single nerve fiber, even those of her feet and her fingers, Nita finally heard footsteps heavily ascend the porch steps. As her heart thudded in her chest, the footsteps crossed the porch and stopped outside the front door.

Raising the shotgun to shoulder level, she heard the squeak the front doorknob always made when you turned it. Just point and pull. The barrel wavered in the dark air before her like the head of a cobra, ready to strike.

But the latch was on; the door would not open.

She listened again as the footsteps climbed slowly down the steps and she saw a shadow pass by the window toward the back of the house.

Faint with fear, Nita sat down on the floor, her back to the front door, her shotgun pointed toward the door to the middle room, and waited. . . .

Henry, still locked in the privy, was kicking the door and yelling like a banshee, while the beam of his flashlight through the cracks in the wood made stripes of light on the grass. And then on the hand outside, covered with blood, which shakily reached for the latch.

"Let me out!" Henry bellowed. "Maaamaaaaa! Help! Mama!"

Suddenly he felt the door give way beneath his kicks, and he watched it swing open silently before him. In a second, without thinking, he was across the space to the house and bounding up the back steps, his light dancing in all directions over the yard.

Behind him he heard the sound of something falling heavily in the grass. What was it? But his terror kept him from flashing his light in that direction. He jerked open the back door and tumbled into the bedroom.

There was Harry still asleep, with the covers pulled up to his chin.

Henry ran to the middle room doorway. Where was Mama? Why was the little light on top of the switchboard off? And the door to the front room closed? He listened for a moment, but all was quiet.

Who had shut him in the privy? He crossed the middle room.

"Mama?" he whispered, as he reached for the doorknob to the front room.

Nita, who had heard the back door open, now watched terrified as the middle room door opened a crack, sending a blinding shaft of light across the floor of the front room toward her.

As the crack widened, she drew in her breath and raised the shotgun again. Took off a fella's head at the neck with it, the Sheriff had said. . . .

With a gasp, she fired!

Henry fell back on the middle room floor, as, with a deafening roar, the door came apart above his head, right where a man's head would've been, showering him with plaster and splinters.

"Mama!" he screamed.

"Henry!" shrieked Nita in sudden panic. "No! Henry!"

She scrambled like a clawing thing to him,

pushing aside the remains of the shattered door. Sobbing uncontrollably, she grabbed him to her bosom. "Henry! My baby!"

Behind them, Harry appeared in his underwear in the doorway to the back room, rubbing his eyes. "Mama?" he said, puzzled.

Bawling and rocking Henry in her lap, she pulled the older boy to her also. "My babies!" she sobbed.

Harry looked up in wonder at the exploded door.

Nita's fear of whatever was outside was forgotten. She had almost shot her own baby, would have if he'd been a little taller, if it'd been Harry, maybe, instead of Henry. How could she have done it? Why hadn't she been thinking?

Through her tears she looked over Harry's bare shoulder to the back door. The hook hung limply on the frame! Not locked!

Scrambling to her feet in the debris of wood and plaster, she rushed to the door. As she reached a shaking hand toward the latch, she heard a faint scratching on the other side of the door.

No! She latched the door and rushed back to the middle room.

Silently, the three of them stood in the center of the floor, listening as the scratching, scratching, continued at the back door.

"Mama," Henry whispered, "somebody locked me in the privy!"

"Mama," Harry whispered, "why'd you shoot a hole in the door?"

"Shhhh!" said Nita, pulling them to her

166

again. "Come on in the front room. Let's sit down."

Slowly, as an hour passed, the three of them sat on the front room linoleum in the hot darkness, listening as the scratching sound became fainter, and then much fainter, almost as if it were a dry leaf caught against the screen or a moth fluttering, dying, in a spider's web at the hinge.

Then it stopped.

And still they sat there, Nita and Harry and Henry, with the now-spent shotgun, sat in the dark on the floor against the sagging couch and watched the back door, motionless, until the sun at last came up.

23

When the early-morning light had warmed the pink walls of the front room enough to fill the air with the sticky vapor of the color, Nita found the courage to release her grip on Henry and straighten out her legs.

She stood up and stepped sideways toward the window the Triplett brothers had talked through. Gingerly, trying not to show her face, she peered out.

The first thing she saw was his boot, lying still in the dust. She leaned a little closer to the window. Arnold's body sprawled grotesquely toward the house. A little farther and she could see his head.

She almost screamed! From temple to chin, his face had been ripped open horribly in a series of bloody gashes. And next to him, teeth up, lay the weapon that had done it: a long-handled, bloody-toothed garden rake.

"Wow!" said Henry, wide-eyed. "Is he dead?" he asked fearfully.

"The pool shooter!" said Harry.

At the front door, Nita pulled back the curtain and looked out. There, on his back under the chinaberry tree, lay the other one, with the yellow handle of a screwdriver protruding from the center of his chest.

"Are they dead, Mama?" Henry repeated.

"Did you kill 'em, Mama?" asked Harry.

She grabbed Henry's hand. "We've got to get out of here," she whispered, as she unlatched the front door. "Come on!"

Fearfully, the three of them stepped slowly off the porch, skirting Calvin's body, not taking their eyes off of it, as if they expected he might pull out the screwdriver and come after them at any moment, and walked toward the road, holding hands.

At the road, they began to run toward Francine Lucas's house, a lady in a blue bathrobe and two little blond boys in their underwear.

24

Within an hour there were several cars parked in front of the Southwest Consolidated Telephone Company's shotgun house, and a dozen or so men stood around in groups of twos and threes in the yard, watching as first Calvin's and then Arnold's bodies were carried away to the waiting ambulance.

Off to one side stood Sheriff Ned Watson, arms folded, with a frown on his face, as Judge Voss's gray Ford pulled up.

"Ned," said the Judge, nodding in greeting.

"Judge, how you?" said the Sheriff, unfolding his arms.

"Mrs. Longley and the boys all right?" Judge Voss asked.

"They're doing Okay. Still a little scared, but who wouldn't be? They're over at the bus station."

"What kinda damn thing went on here, anyway?" the Judge asked.

"Well," said Sheriff Watson, scratching his head, "these two was a couple no-goods, drunks, you know, trouble-makers. Way I figure it, old Bailey . . ."

"Old Bailey?" asked Judge Voss.

"Yeah," nodded the Sheriff. "Look back here." He led the way to the back stoop where the handyman's body lay in a pool of drying blood, the hand extending to the door screen.

"Kinda a yard man around here, mowed lawns, odd jobs, that sorta work. Been around here, oh say, about two years. Gimped-up leg and face *all* messed up. Looked like pure-D hell. Nice enough fella, though, if you could get past his looks."

"Ned," interrupted the Judge, "you gonna tell me some crippled-up yard man put those two away?"

"Damn if he didn't!" grinned the Sheriff. "Got 'em both. Hit one of 'em with a rake, over yonder by the side of the house." He pointed in the direction of the window. "The sonofabitch had him a stack of wood and some old papers piled up. Gonna burn the house flat down, by the looks of it . . . after they done their business with Mrs. Longley.

"The other one, he got the other one out there under that little old chinaberry tree. Poked him in the chest with a yaller-handled Phillips screwdriver about . . . yay long." He held his hands about a foot apart. "Made a little round hole no bigger'n duck shot. Did the job, though, by God. Killed him flat out.

"'Course old Bailey got it, too. Three times in the belly with a K-Bar pocket knife. He made

171

it around to the back of the house here, bleeding all over the place.

She heard him, Mrs. Longley, but 'course she
wasn't about to open that door. Had them two
little boys in there with her. Hell, I don't blame
her, Judge. No way I'd'a opened that door. I
mean, if I was a woman . . . with two little
boys . . ."

The Judge nodded.

"Anyway, old Bailey, he bled to death right
here. . . . Look where he scratched the paint
plumb off the screen."

Sadly the Judge nodded again. He looked up
as a man approached around the corner of the
house.

"Judge, you know my deputy?" Sheriff Watson asked.

"How you doing, Clint?" said the Judge,
shaking the deputy's hand.

"Aw, I got me a damn summer cold," the
deputy sniffed. "Can't seem to shake it off."

"He's sick half the time," snorted the Sheriff.

"Aw hell, I ain't neither."

"You go out to Bailey's shack?" Sheriff Watson asked.

"Sure did," the deputy answered. "Didn't find
a thing. Couple cans of Vienna sausages and
some light bread was about all. No identifica-
tion."

He reached into his shirt pocket. "This is all
we found in his overalls." He handed the Sheriff
a small white card.

The Sheriff turned the card over and studied
it a moment.

"Let me have a look at that, Ned," said Judge Voss, reaching for the card.

The Sheriff handed it over.

"Oh yeah," said the Deputy, rubbing at his nose with a blue plaid handkerchief, "call come in on the radio a minute ago. Dead Meskin over on the other side of town. Head all bashed in with a 2 x 4."

The Sheriff looked up incredulous. "Meskin?" he repeated.

"Yep," sniffed Clint. "The one that ran the bar, you know, the fat one. Got his house all tore to hell too, and his wife and kids is hysterical. Ain't been able to tell nobody nothing about it."

The Judge looked at the face of the cards the Sheriff had handed him—a photograph, frayed and bent from being carried in a pocket a long time. He studied it, puzzled. Something strange . . .

The wind grabbed the picture from his fingers and blew it toward the road among the weeds.

"Hell, let it go," said Sheriff Watson. "It don't tell us nothing."

"Come on, Clint," he said, motioning toward Mr. Bailey's body. "Let's get 'im outta here.

"We gotta git on over to that Meskin's house, see what that mess's all about."

The Judge was still looking at the card where it had lodged in the brush.

"You know, Judge," said the Sheriff, "I been Sheriff here—what?—twenty-something years and this here—Bailey and the two drunks and

173

now dead Meskin—that's more *corpus delecti*'s than I seen in all those years put together."

"It don't rain but it pours, huh? Let's go, Clint."

25

It was hard for Harry to believe that everything they owned was in those few parcels
beside them on the bus station curb: the
pile of boxes, the two old suitcases tied with
rope, and the small tin suitcase. Everything,
that is, except for the red wagon and the bat-
tered blue bicycle he had almost learned to
ride. There wouldn't be room for them on the
bus, and Mama had promised to get them a
new wagon and a new bike after they got to
Wichita Falls.

"Hello, Jean," said Nita warmly. Mrs. Lester
stood holding her baby, waiting for the bus
with her mother and two of her husband's
sisters and his father.

"Oh, Nita," Jean Lester cried. "Today! Jack's
coming home today!"

In a minute, when the bus came around the
corner, Harry could see a wooden crutch waving from one of the windows.

"There he is!" cried one of the sisters, as all the relatives surged forward.

"Oh, Jack!" Jean whispered.

Private Jack Lester, tall and thin in his uniform, hobbled down from the big bus on his one leg and his crutch, grinning and laughing.

Jean, in tears, kissed him, as did the two sisters. His father shook his hand and clapped him on the back, and Jean's mother handed him the baby.

Harry watched as the daddy lifted the tiny son he had never seen, lifted him high over his head by the arms and then hugged him tightly to his chest.

"Daddy's home!" Jack Lester kissed the baby on the cheek.

With an ache in his throat, Harry turned away.

"Is it time to get on the bus yet, Mama?" he asked.

His mind fumbled with the stack of things that had happened in the last two days, shuffling through them, looking for one that wouldn't make him want to cry when he thought about it; the fight with the pool shooters; the fight with the Jap in the yard when Mama got so mad; the broken egg basket; Teddy leaving them; getting into the car on the highway and driving away; the sudden, startling news that they were moving, to a place he'd never heard of far to the north, Wichita Falls; having to tell Mr. Bailey goodbye, knowing somehow they'd never see him again . . .

He shuddered, remembering last night— hiding in the front room in the dark with the middle room door all shot to pieces and Henry and Mama both crying. And this morning— the two pool shooters dead in the yard, blood and awfulness, and there, beside the back door, Mr. Bailey, poor Mr. Bailey, the only friend they had left. . . .

He wished he could go to sleep and forget it all and find out when he woke up that it had all been a bad dream. But he examined the cut on his finger and, remembering the taste of his blood, knew it had all really happened.

"Bye, Jean," called Nita, as she moved the boys toward the bus, but Mrs. Lester, laughing and talking and hugging her husband, didn't hear.

After Nita spoke with the bus driver about the boxes and suitcases, the three of them climbed on the bus and settled into their seats, Henry sitting on Nita's lap by the window and Harry next to them by the aisle.

No one said anything as the bus lumbered into gear and lurched out of the station.

The Lester family was climbing into two old cars, laughing and joking. Jack Lester's father put the crutch in the back seat.

Suddenly Harry was aware of the bulge the heavy Masonic ring made in his pocket. The ring Mr. Bailey had given them! He pulled it out and looked at it.

That was funny! There was something he hadn't noticed before: three initials engraved inside the band. Turning it to the light, he tried to read them: W.R.L.

"Mama," he said, closing his fingers around the ring again, "what does W.R.L. stand for?"

"W.R.L.?" said Nita, turning toward him from the window.

"Yes, ma'am," Harry turned the ring in the palm of his hand.

"Well," said Nita after a moment, looking out the window again, "those were your daddy's initials. . . ."

Harry opened his fingers and looked at the ring in amazement. Suddenly there were tears in his eyes. Mr. Bailey!

"Why?" asked Nita, looking down at him.

Not answering, Harry curled his fingers tightly around the warm metal, squeezing it lovingly. *Daddy*.

"Harry?" asked Nita.

"I was just wondering, Mama." He tried to smile at her.

Putting her arm around him, Nita pulled him close.

As the bus turned down the road that went past the shotgun house, Harry leaned over to get one last look out the window. The cars and the men were gone now.

Henry pointed to the old blue bike.

Harry said goodbye to it. Under the chinaberry tree lay the upturned red wagon. Harry said goodbye to both of them. Goodbye to the porch and the privy. Goodbye to the cow in the vacant lot. Goodbye to the horse on the ceiling. Goodbye to all this.

The small white card, the one from Mr. Bailey's pocket that the breeze had spun out of the Judge's fingers into the grass by the road, flipped over as the bus thundered by, lifted by the dust from the passing wheels, and landed face-up, a frayed-edged wallet-sized photograph, in the bushy weeds of the vacant lot.

When the dust had settled and Harry had finished saying goodbyes, the three faces in the picture smiled up at the screaming cicadas under the bright blue sky. The man proudly balancing the chunky, laughing baby on his shoulder and holding tight the hand of a little blond-haired boy of about three, who was grinning the happiest grin of all.

As the bus swayed down the road toward the highway, Harry sat back in his seat and rotated the smooth warm ring in his palm. A secret, happy smile, not at all unlike the one on the face of the boy in the photograph, spread across his face as he closed his eyes and nestled close to Nita.

His daddy had come back after all.

SPECIAL PREVIEW

William D. Wittliff
and Sara Clark

Thaddeus Rose and Eddie

Based on the screenplay by
William D. Wittliff

Introducing an exciting new American story-teller, William D. Wittliff, whose magic is as apparent on the screen as it is on the printed page. His authentic and moving portrayal of people and places is so exact and so perceptive that you'll find yourself living in that place and time, and feeling the heartbreak and hilarity of his characters.

Thaddeus Rose sucked in his stomach and tightened his belt another notch. He turned his left side to the bathroom mirror: no beer belly yet. Though most of his Texan neighbors displayed theirs like cultured pearls, he knew there wasn't a woman alive, that, given her choice, would pick fat. And he wasn't interested in the ones that didn't have a choice. He narrowed his eyes and appraised his conformation from the right side. Stud, goddawg!

He had already thumbed the last button into place on his best blue-plaid western shirt, and had inspected the faded collar, frayed from rubbing against his sun-reddened neck on an awful lot of Saturday nights. And, he smiled to himself, from rubbing against the soft and scented necks of the women he'd managed to grab and hold onto a good many of those Saturday nights.

Closely interrogating first his left temple and then his right, he searched his dark hair for signs of gray. Not bad. Could easily pass for forty-five, if they didn't have their glasses on or weren't looking too close. They'd never guess fifty-six. He ran the comb under the tap and, knocking off the largest drops of water against the grimy basin, expertly arched his hair into a high-winged pompadour, bending his six-feet-two a little to see in the mirror as he sculpted the top.

"Yore cheatin' hawurt wiyell teyell on

yeeeewwww!" he sang, wincing as he twirled a wooden matchstick first in his left ear and then in his right. Why couldn't he ever remember any more words to that song? he wondered, frowning at the cracks and scuffs in his faithful boots. Vaseline'd do it. He glossed the jelly over the ancient leather, covering the worst scars and adding a shine. The last of it he cleaned off his hands by running his big fingers through his hair.

Unrolling the end of the brown paper sack he kept on the closet shelf, he took out his almost new pearly-gray Stetson hat. He set it very carefully on his head and pulled it down at an experimentally rakish angle over one eye, judging the result in the mirror. Not quite. With a hand on either side of the brim, he cocked it forward a little more and tilted his head back, smiling devilishly to test the effect.

Drawing a little closer to the mirror, he flashed another, more seductive smile, lowering his eyelids and parting his lips just slightly. That was good. Or from the side: He turned his left profile to the mirror and cut a sidelong glance with a wicked leer. From the front again, he cocked one big shoulder higher than the other and grinned disarmingly.

But his teeth. He examined them closely: too stained. Licking his index finger, he stuck it into the open box of baking soda on the shelf by the basin and scrubbed back and forth across his front teeth. He rinsed his mouth with water from his cupped hand and bared his teeth again in a dazzle of white. Better.

He dried his hands on his Levis and cocked

his head back to grin crinkly eyed at himself once more. Hunting, that's what he and Eddie always called it.

"Hey, boy," he said with a wink, "think you're gonna catch one tonight?"

It was only inside his own house, the house he'd grown up in, that he ever thought of himself as "Thaddeus." The minute he stepped outside his door, he became the name almost everybody in Allison had always known him by: "Sledge." So it was Sledge Rose who steered his old brown pickup between the chugholes in the dirt road, while the wooden sides on the truck's bed clattered in time to the radio announcer droning the wholesale prices of farm products and livestock.

It had been a warm enough day for November, but now that the sun was dipping in and out of the hilltop cedar breaks in the rockstrewn field his friend Eddie called a pasture, the shadows were chillier than he'd expected. Old Eddie, he thought, *and a Saturday night*!

In the rear-view mirror he could see the dust powdering the shafts of late sunlight between the flaming red sumacs that lined the road, hanging there like something painted into the Hill Country landscape, as much a part of it as the long-boned limestone, fractured and scattered with grass seed, and the stands of brown scrub oak that clung to the thin soil.

He had noticed before that every season in the Hill Country had its colors. Fall was red and brown and orange, like this. Spring was always meadow pinks and bluebonnets, and summer in the heat had been green and yellow from daisies and sunflowers, the mesquite, and goldenrod. Winter, when it came, would be various shades of gray: brown-gray in the bark of the leafless oaks, green-gray in the frost-bitten grass, blue-gray in the heavy skies and the icy rains.

As he dodged his way through a rocky wash in the road, a splash of movement beside a twisted, peeling, red-barked madroña suddenly became a huge deer leaping across the clearing from a little stand of cedar, as if shot from a hillside cannon. A buck, gray, with a fine spread of antlers.

Damn. Sledge slammed the pickup to a dead stop and cut the ignition. In a second, he had grabbed his .30-.30 lever-action Winchester from the rack behind his head and, resting his elbow on the window, brought the running buck into his sight. Must be sixteen or eighteen points at least—a lot of deer, a lot of years. The cross-hairs just above the shoulder: It was an easy kill.

But before Sledge could squeeze off the shot, the old buck stopped. He lifted his huge head and gazed, unafraid, straight into the rifle's sight. Sledge drew in his breath. What the hell? He could see the deer's eyes, large and luminous as lanterns, staring at him, no, into him, through him, beyond him. Sledge felt the hairs on his arms and the back of his neck prickling. He lifted his face from the rifle and stared fearfully back at the deer. In all his years of hunting, he had never felt this way. What was the matter?

Casting him a last penetrating look, the

buck broke and ran toward a little clump of wild persimmons. Sledge relaxed his grip on the rifle and watched, strangely disturbed. Somehow, he could almost feel his own cloven hoof against that limestone reef, his own brandished horn scraping those leafless twigs, as the buck reached the shadow of the trees.

And then, without warning, in the split-second before he flinched at the crack of the high-powered deer rifle, Sledge saw his buck crash to the ground, knocked heavily onto his side, his four feet splayed stiffly to the wind and his antlers digging into the stony dirt.

Slack-handed and gape-mouthed, Sledge focused uncomprehendingly on the inert gray lump on the ragged ground, the sticklike leg jutting into the dry grass. He felt his own neck jerk when the leg jerked, once. And he jerked again when a burst of bright red windbreaker, a hunter, stepped from the scrub oak, rifle in hand, and approached the deer.

City man, Sledge realized, as his mind began to function again, noting the red jacket and shiny orange hunting cap with its earflaps tied over the crown. City man killed my deer. He let out a long shaky breath and watched as the hunter drew a big knife and began to cut the musk glands from the buck's hind legs.

When Sledge turned to put his rifle back in the rack, he realized his hands were trembling. What was the matter? Just a dead deer. Happens all the time, every year. He took one last look and turned on the ignition.

At the sound of the truck engine, the hunter looked up from his work. Sledge dropped the car into low gear and eased on down the road. He put first a big cedar, then a clump of mesquite, then a dip into a bone-dry water crossing, and then a little hill, blood-red with sumacs, between himself and the vision of the big, gray buck. It was almost enough.

Eddie, he tried to think, and Saturday night.

Sledge turned the pickup into Eddie's rutted driveway. There sat Eddie, swinging his short legs off the porch, which listed to the front of his elaborately patchworked three-room house. Scraps of weathered boards, patches of tarpaper and rags of canvas, flattened beer cans, and a discarded hubcap or two, added over the years, held Eddie's house together. There was even an entire five-sign Burma Shave jingle he'd stolen years ago from the highway to Austin and tacked over various splits and gaps. Gave the place class, he said, having some literature around.

Sledge's pickup bounced past the disintegrating Model T truck that had been slowly returning its rusting iron and rotting rubber to the surrounding dust near Eddie's cow pens for thirty-odd years. It lived on now in a new incarnation: About half of Eddie's flock of scrawny chickens roosted in it every night. A few enterprising hens had scratched out nesting places in the excelsior of the disintegrating seat, and a contented cackle rose even now from its musty interior.

Sledge slowed his pickup to a stop beside the faded and dented blue '46 Chevy, which slouched under the chinaberry tree next to the porch. The last ray of the setting sun glinted off the smooth chrome breasts of a winged girl poised tippy-toe on the point of the Chevy's hood. Eddie called her Lena Ann.

Sledge honked a defective little beep with his horn: *beeeeeiiiip, beeeeeiiiip.*

"Come on, Eddie!" he whooped. "Let's go catch a pretty girl!"

Grinning like a possum in a red-striped cowboy shirt, Eddie pulled his hat wickedly down over one eye, winked at Sledge, and jumped off the porch. Smaller than Sledge, with a feisty gleam that was almost boyish (though he was only a year younger than Sledge), Eddie had kept Sledge laughing for as long as he could remember.

As Eddie reached for the doorhandle to Sledge's truck, his mangy brown dog did what Sledge had expected him to do the minute Eddie'd put a foot on the ground. With a growl like a kamikaze and a furious snap of jaws, he leaped from under the Chevy and fastened on Eddie's pantsleg, tugging and snarling.

"Damn you, Dog!" Eddie yelled angrily, swatting at the animal with his hat. "Get outta here!" With his free leg he kicked the dog away. "You damn fool dog!"

"Git 'im, Dog!" Sledge laughed. "Git the ol' bastard!"

Glowering, Eddie slammed the pickup door and Dog broke once again into his fury of growls and barks, bounding and snapping at the window like a shark in a feeding frenzy. Sledge spun the pickup into reverse, scattering chickens across the yard, as Dog raced to keep up his attack.

"Damn you, Dog! Ain't you got no sense at all?" Eddie hollered. "Git on now!" He examined the rip in his pantsleg.

Sledge turned the truck back down the driveway, steering it above the deepest ruts, presenting the still-chasing dog a mouthful of exhaust-laden dust. "You must enjoy the hell outta that dog," he laughed.

Eddie rolled his blue eyes and replaced his hat at its jaunty angle. "Saturday!" he said.

"Damn right!" cried Sledge, turning on the radio just as Patsy Cline moaned the last words of "This Is the Thaaaaanks Ah Git fer Lovin' Yeeeeewwwww."

"Awh-hawh!" Eddie hollered, as the plinky-plink music of the Alvin Karl Real Estate ad started. Hell, Sledge thought, every damn time you turn on the radio.

"Hidy! Howyew?" the radio blared. *"I'm Alvin Karl, President, Alvin Karl Real Estate."*

Plinky-plink went the music, as two girls with nasal twang sang to the tune of "Skip to My Lou": *"Alvin Karl, he sells Texas. Alvin Karl, he sells Texas."*

Sledge made a loud raspberry, but Eddie joined in the singing: *"Alvin Karl, he sells Texas. Won't yew come in an' say hiiiii-dy!"*

Alvin Karl began his spiel: *"Fella come in one day, said . . ."*

And a second voice, cracked with pain, began: *"Howdy, Alvin. . . . Down on my luck. . . . Wife left. . . . Kids gone bad."*

Eddie was repeating his troubles right along

with him. *"Ain't got nothin' left but two World War I Army trucks."*

"Tell yew what I did, folks," Alvin Karl's voice broke in. *"Took those trucks on trade for a little piece o' land on the Perdanales River. Now he's fishin' ever' mornin' an' thankin' me an' the Lord ever' evenin'."*

Eddie knew every word of it.

Sledge'd never met a real estate agent, and he didn't think he'd like to. He reached to turn off the radio.

Eddie grabbed his hand. "We ain't done!" he cried.

"It started with a hidy an' it changed that fella's life an' fortune!" Alvin Karl chortled. *"I always got somethin' to sell or trade. Always lookin' for somethin' to buy. Alvin Karl Real Estate. Highway 281. San Antonio."*

As the duet chanted the last line of the song again, *"Why don't yew come in an' say hiiiidy!"* and the plinky-plink music faded away, Sledge flicked the radio off.

"Hell, Eddie," he laughed, "you oughta see if he'll take your Model T chicken coop for some lakefront up at Marble Falls."

Eddie giggled. "Hidy, Alvin," he intoned, exactly like the voice in the ad, "Down on my luck. . . . Wife won't leave. . . . Kids are goody-goodies. . . . "

Sledge whooped. Old Eddie—always left him laughing.

Dear Reader:

The Pinnacle Books editors strive to select and produce books that are exciting, entertaining and readable . . . no matter what the category. From time to time we will attempt to discover what you, the reader, think about a particular book.

Now that you've finished reading *Raggedy Man*, we'd like to find out what you liked, or didn't like, about this story. We'll share your opinions with the author and discuss them as we plan future books. This will result in books that you will find more to your liking. As in fine art and good cooking a matter of taste is involved; and for you, of course, it is *your* taste that is most important to you. For William Wittliff, Sara Clark, and the Pinnacle editors, it is not the critics' reviews and awards that have been most rewarding, it is the unending stream of readers' mail. Here is where we discover what readers like, what they *feel* about a story, and what they find memorable. So, do help us in becoming a little better in providing you with the kind of stories you like. Here's how . . .

WIN BOOKS . . . AND $200!

Please fill out the following pages and mail them as indicated. Every week, for twelve weeks following publication, the editors will choose, at random, a reader's name from all the questionnaires received. The twelve lucky readers will receive $25 worth of paperbacks *and* become an official entry in our 1979 Pinnacle Books Reader Sweepstakes. The winner of this sweepstakes drawing will receive a Grand Prize of $200, the inclusion of their name in a forthcoming Pinnacle Book (as a special acknowledgment, possibly even as a character!), and several other local prizes to be announced to each initial winner. As a further inducement to send in your questionnaire *now*, we will also send the first 25 replies received a free book by return mail! Here's a chance to talk to the author and editor, voice your opinions, and win some great prizes, too!

—The Editors

READER SURVEY

NOTE:- Please feel free to expand on any of these questions on a separate page, or to express yourself on any aspect of your thoughts on reading . . . but do be sure to include this entire questionnaire with any such letters.

---

1. Are you glad you bought this book, and did it live up to your expectations?

---

2. What was it about this book that induced you to buy it?

   (A. The title_____) (B. The author's name_____)

   (C. A friend's recommendation_____)

   (D. The cover art_____)

   (E. The cover description_____)

   (F. Subject matter_____) (G. Advertisement_____)

   (H. Heard author on TV or radio_____)

   (I. Read a previous book by author_____ . . . which one? _____)

   (J. Bookstore display_____)

   (K. Other? _____)

3. What is the book you read just before this one?

   And how would you rate it with *Raggedy Man*?

   ---

4. What is the very next book you plan to read?

_____

How did you decide on that? _____

5. Where did you buy *Raggedy Man*? _____

_____

(Name and address of store, please):

_____

_____

6. Where do you buy the majority of your paper-backs? _____

7. What seems to be the major factor that per-suades you to buy a certain book?

_____

8. How many books do you buy each month?

_____

9. Do you ever write letters to the author or pub-lisher . . . and why? _____

_____

10. About how many hours a week do you spend reading books? _____ How many hours a week watching television? _____

11. What other spare-time activity do you enjoy most? _____ For how many hours a week? _____

12. Which magazines do you read regularly? . . . in order of your preference _____,

_____, _____,

_____

13. Of your favorite magazine, what is it that you like best about it? _____
_____

14. What is your favorite television show of the past year or so? _____

15. What is your favorite motion picture of the past year or so? _____

16. What is the most disappointing television show you've seen lately? _____

17. What is the most disappointing motion picture you've seen lately? _____

18. What is the most disappointing book you've read lately? _____

19. Are there authors that you like so well that you read *all* their books? _____
Who are they? _____

20. And can you explain *why* you like their books so much? _____
_____
_____

21. Which particular books by these authors do you like best? _____
_____

22. Did you read Taylor Caldwell's *Captains and the Kings?*____ Did you watch it on television? ____ Which did you do first? _____

23. Did you read John Jakes' *The Bastard?* ____ Did you watch it on TV?____ Which first?____

Have you read any of the other books in John Jakes' Bicentennial Series? _____
What do you think of them? _____

24. Did you read James Michener's *Centennial*?_____
Did you watch it on TV?_____ Which first?_____

25. Did you read Irwin Shaw's *Rich Man, Poor Man*? _____ Did you watch it on TV? _____
Which first? _____

26. Of all the recent books you've read, or films you've seen, are there any that you would compare in any way to *Raggedy Man*? _____

27. Do you think any of Wittliff and Clark's characters were based on real people? If so, who reminded you of whom? _____
_____
_____
_____
_____

28. Rank the following descriptions of *Raggedy Man* as you feel they are best defined:

	Excellent	*Okay*	*Poor*
A. A sense of reality	____	____	____
B. Suspense	____	____	____
C. Intrigue	____	____	____
D. Sexuality	____	____	____
E. Violence	____	____	____
F. Romance	____	____	____
G. History	____	____	____

H. Characterization   ———   ———   ———

I. Scenes, events   ———   ———   ———

J. Pace, readability   ———   ———   ———

K. Dialogue   ———   ———   ———

L. Style   ———   ———   ———

29. Have you read *Thaddeus Rose & Eddie*? ———

_____

30. Have you read any books by Howard Fast? ———
Which ones? _____

31. Have you read any books by James Michener?
——— Which ones? _____

32. Have you read any books by John Jakes? ———
Which ones? _____

33. In *Raggedy Man*, which character did you find
most fascinating? _____
Most likeable? ——— Most exciting? ——— Least
interesting? ———Which one did you identify
with most? ———————

34. Do you have any thoughts regarding the length
of this book? ——— Would you have liked it to
be longer? ——— Shorter? ———

35. Would you be interested in a sequel to *Raggedy
Man*? _____

36. Would you be interested in reading a similar
story, but in a different locale? ——— Where, for
example? _____

_____

37. Do you like to read about people involved in international finance? _____ Government and politics? _____ The "jet-set"? _____ Show business? _____ Small town events? _____

38. What, in your opinion, is the best or most vivid scene in *Raggedy Man*? _____
_____

39. Did you find any errors or other upsetting things in this book? _____
_____

40. What do you do with your paperbacks after you've read them? _____
_____

41. Do you buy paperbacks in any of the following categories, and approximately how many do you buy in a year?

A. Contemporary fiction (like *this* book) _____
B. Historical romance _____
C. Family saga _____
D. Romance (like Harlequin) _____
E. Romantic suspense _____
F. Gothic romance _____
G. Occult novels _____
H. War novels _____
I. Action/adventure novels _____
J. "Bestsellers" _____
K. Science fiction _____
L. Mystery _____

M. Westerns   ——

N. Nonfiction   ——

O. Biography   ——

P. How-To books   ——

Q. Other _____

42. And, lastly, some profile data on *you* the reader . . .

    A. Age: 12–16____ 17–20____ 21–30____
            31–40____ 41–50____ 51–60____
            61 or over____

    B. Occupation: _____

    C. Education level; check last grade completed:
       10____ 11____ 12____ Freshman____
       Sophomore____ Junior____ Senior____
       Graduate School____, plus any specialized
       schooling _____

    D. Your average annual gross income: Under
       $10,000____ $10,000–$15,000____
       $15,000–$20,000____ $20,000–
       $30,000____ $30,000–$50,000____
       Above $50,000____

    E. Did you read a lot as a child?____ Do you
       recall your favorite childhood novel? ____
       _____

    F. Do you find yourself reading more or less
       than you did five years ago?__

    G. Do you read hardcover books?____ How
       often?____ If so, are they books that you

buy?_____ borrow?_____ or trade?_____ Or other?_____

H. Does the imprint (Pinnacle, Avon, Bantam, etc.) make any difference to you when considering a paperback purchase? _____

I. Have you ever bought paperbacks by mail directly from the publisher?_____ And do you like to buy books that way? _____

J. Would you be interested in buying paperbacks via a book club or subscription program?_____ And, in your opinion, what would be the best reasons for doing so? _____ _____ . . . the problems in doing so? _____

K. Is there something that you'd like to see writers or publishers do for you as a reader of paperbacks? _____
_____

THANK YOU FOR TAKING THE TIME TO REPLY TO THIS, THE FIRST PUBLIC READER SURVEY IN PAPERBACK HISTORY!

NAME _____ PHONE_____
ADDRESS _____
CITY _____ STATE _____ ZIP _____

Please return this questionnaire to:

The Editors; Survey Dept. RM
Pinnacle Books, Inc.
2029 Century Park East
Los Angeles, CA 90067